Praise For *Paperboy*

"*Paperboy* is fun and blissfully irreverent. The sheer density of the humor had me smiling as I sat back and let the voice flow over me. I find it difficult to imagine that *Paperboy* would not be universally enjoyed by everyone who reads it."

--Greg Tripodi, Author

"Hayen is a humorist in the spirit of David Sedaris, with a satirical, laugh-out-loud voice. It's one part comedic rant and one part genuine heart. This book is for anyone who has ever tried to understand humanity. Well done, my man."

--Annabelle Lewis, Author

"Poignant and funny. Captures and dissects human behaviors in many clever ways. The multi-layer humor is priceless. *Paperboy* is like a bristly brush for my brain. Awesome."

--Karl Jorgenson, Author

"Glenn Hayen is an expert observer of the human life. He writes with a rhythm of heightened speech and unapologetic, tongue-in-cheek irreverence, perfectly suited for dissecting life's absurdities."

--JJ Harrigan, Author

Paperboy

Glenn Hayen

Every word within this book has been written by a human.

All characters and events depicted are fictional.

The author values and supports copyright. Copyright encourages creativity, promotes free speech, and creates a vibrant culture.

Thank you for complying with copyright laws by not reproducing, scanning, or distributing any part of it in any form nor uploaded to any website, database, language-learning model, or repository, retrieval, or artificial intelligence, or system without the author's permission.

Originally published 2026

ISBN: 978-1964354101

Library of Congress Catalog Card Number:

2026904238

For Carissa, Phillip, Todd

"Maybe to understand mankind, we have to look at the word itself; "Mankind". Basically, it's made up of two separate words- "mank" and "ind".

--Jack Handey

PART 1
PAPER ROUTE

We were a Catholic family. An ethnic European mix with a hint of Puerto Rican. My dad was a serial killer. Not people. That family legacy ended with my great grandfather. No, Dad was a serial job killer. And his job slayings created some domestic financial stress.

As for Mom, well, she tried. But, alas, she had a tendency to drink. Daily. Boy she liked her wine. But as I think about it, she also had a soft spot for beer, vodka, gin, whiskey, brandy. She was pretty much an equal opportunity drinker before there was equal opportunity. A trail blazer you might say.

My estimate is I had about fourteen siblings. The reason for the uncertainty is some departed before my arrival and some arrived after my departure. But I met most and knew a few of them.

I was a complex kid. A blend of wimp, with nerdish tendencies, easily confused, a tad lazy, with marginal athletic skills, and a poor student. But I wasn't perfect.

There's more, but that's probably enough.

We lived in a mid-sized Midwest city in a neighborhood called Sacred Heart.

Long ago, Sacred Heart was vacant land behind Andy's Tavern. Owner Andy had a friend, Father Dave, a Catholic assistant church pastor and a frequent tavern patron. Andy's was far enough away from Father Dave's current parish employer for him to imbibe while avoiding his parishioners.

One day while sipping sacred wine together, Andy shared his dream to build houses on his vacant property. Father Dave said he dreamed of building a church and school. Thus began their discussion of a potential joint venture to achieve those dreams.

The plan was Andy would provide to Dave the land. Dave would convince the diocese to invest into building the church and school and pay Andy rent. The church and school would drive demand for the houses. The houses would drive demand for the church and school. Each contributes to the success of both.

Andy admitted his ignorance of how Father Dave could pay the rent. The padre then shared details of the Catholic business model.

Collection plates at Mass are a staple. But tithing is more significant. And service fees even more so. Fees for funerals, baptisms, first communions, confirmations, marriages. Marriage annulments are a huge windfall and exorcisms are a great cash infusion.

And when the houses are built, house blessing fees would go right to the bottom line. Concluding, Dave said there might also be some revenue opportunities from services performed within the tavern.

Andy was both stunned and impressed. "Holy mackerel, Dave."

"Oh, bless you, Andy. Every parish does cod for the Friday fish fry. Mackerel can differentiate us and charge a premium. Now that's thinking outside the box. Or should I say, thinking outside the fish?"

"Stop it, Dave. You crack me up."

Their verbal agreement was blessed by Father Dave, and celebrated with a shot of Christian Brothers Brandy. Sacred Heart gave birth to houses on twelve streets, a church and a school, and the Catholic families moved in.

Although much of life success is about good decisions, luck is shortchanged for accolades. And boy was I lucky. In 1960, just before my tenth birthday, my mom got me a paper route. I don't know how she did that. Paper route demand seriously exceeded the supply.

My introduction to the job was delivered by Mr. Patrick "Mully" Mulldoon from the *Daily Herald Tribune Times Star Journal.* He sat with me and Mom at our kitchen table as he went over the job responsibilities.

There were three basic duties:

1. Deliver the papers to subscriber customers seven days per week. The weekday afternoon edition before 5 PM; the weekend morning paper before 8:30 AM.
2. Collect payments for the papers from each customer every Monday and Tuesday before 8:30 PM.
3. Bring payments to the downtown newspaper office every Saturday before noon.

Following his duty instructions, Mr. Mulldoon then shifted focus to address the seriousness of my role. At that point, I started to mentally drift a tad, but his message was something about being more important than the Pony Express. Which I thought wasn't much of a stretch, given the Pony Express was obsolete. But he stressed my job was critical because I was responsible for bringing the world news into my customers' world.

Now it wasn't the content of his message that resonated with me. It was his delivery. Mr. Mulldoon had slipped into an almost reverent tone for his brief speech. He had created a spiritual like aura within our tiny kitchen. And upon his conclusion, an awkward silence fell. Broken when Mom turned to me and added "remember, never be rude." Mom was a rude stickler. I could get away with most behaviors if I wasn't rude. Anyway, Mom then blessed herself. Feeling pressure to participate, I said "amen." And then Mully left.

I was replacing Bob Zelinski, retiring at age 16. I shadowed him for a week as he showed me the ropes. Bob was a nice guy and professional. At the conclusion to my OJT, he gave me his wire cutters, extra rubber bands, two Liberty Bell logo imprinted heavy fabric shoulder strapped newspaper bags, money collection bag, and customer receipt binder. He wished me luck.

The paper route was a large step for me; a huge undertaking. Might even be considered brobdingnabian. Until then, my responsibilities were minimal. Get dressed and get to school on time. My track record for both was spotty.

But I felt ready to fill Bob's shoes. Until that first day solo. When the wire wrapped newspaper bundles were dumped on my front sidewalk. And I realized that I already missed Bob. But Bob's former customers would soon miss him more.

I had responsibility for four of Sacred Heart's twelve residential streets. There were eighty-eight houses and eighty-eight customers. Because every house subscribed to the newspaper. Maybe because of the inherent value of the paper. Or perhaps it was a requirement for either citizenship or, maybe a prerequisite for living in the neighborhood. I'm not sure. But anyway, it was helpful because I didn't have to keep track of which houses were subscribers.

My customers were a collection of "mostlys." Mostly white skinned with mostly blue collars. Mostly Irish, Italian, Polish. Mostly Catholic. Mostly dad, mom and kids.

Kids mostly played. Moms mostly yelled at kids, cooked, cleaned, shopped. Dads mostly worked, mostly at factories. Mostly equal wealth, mostly slightly below average, mostly TV's within mostly small houses with mostly small porches on mostly small lots and mostly a used car parked on mostly graveled small driveways mostly without a garage.

Despite their mostly similarities, each of my customers were different. As I learned trundling house-to-house through my small urban jungle. Every family was unique as snowflakes. But to truly capture that snowflake uniqueness required my detailed observation.

So, was I a sponge for detail? Maybe, but unlikely. More likely my awareness was a result of my frequent visits. For six years, three weeks, I delivered their newspaper seven days per week. Once a week I collected payment from each.

Here's my paper route math—I made 2,527 visits to each house. Even with my tendency to miss the obvious, with that many renditions, something had to resonate; something about each of them had to make a lasting contribution into my memory bank.

And that is what I'll share. Oh, one more detail before I rudely neglect, my name is Tom.

ST. ANDY AVENUE

Lebowski

The Lebowski family, like many customers, had a lot of kids. Sally, my age, was a nice, smart, pretty girl whom I really liked and was trying to figure out how she might like me.

Previously I said my dad had many jobs. But only one directly involved me.

Briefly in fifth grade, Dad delivered bar snacks to taverns. These snacks included various kinds of chips, nuts, popcorn, pretzels, and beef jerky. And some disgusting things that floated in large jars of murky fluids—eggs, pickles, pickled pigs' feet—stuff that seemed more appropriate in a toilet than a stomach.

During this tavern delivery stint, mornings before school, I helped load these items into his truck. The pay was poor. Actually, there was no pay. But it did provide my breakfast. Except for the murky fluid contents, I sampled the entire menu before I settled upon my favorite-Slim Jims. These were little greasy sausages that slid easily out of their wrapper housing and easily slid into my gut. They tasted great and were filling, really stuck to my ribs.

And, unfortunately, stuck to my breath. As I learned from Sally one morning before school. Standing next to her, Sally said "P.U.", what have you been eating?" "Slim Jims" I proudly replied. "What's a Slim Jim?" "Well, I began, "they're sort of like… oh, never mind." I thought, how do I even begin to explain the nuance of a Slim Jim?

For breakfast the next morning I decided to pass on my Slim Jim favorite and ate some pork rinds, not my favorite, but a positive Sally breath test warranted this sacrifice.

At school, I went up to Sally, blew into her face and asked what she thought. She said better. What did you eat? Pork rinds, I replied. What's a pork rind, she asked. I thought Sally seemed to be a little sheltered. Or were all girls? Anyway, rather than explain a pork rind, I told her why don't I bring you one the next day.

A good and perhaps lucky move on my part, because Sally liked the pork rind. And maybe she was starting to like me. Alas, our breathtaking romance was brief and became breathless shortly later. I don't remember why because I didn't know why. Maybe what we had was less romance and more like speed dating. Disappointing sure, but a learning experience. Slim Jims won't win a girl's heart, but pork rinds might.

Arronni

Mr. Arronni wasn't Superman, but he was a man of steel. He was a steel-making man at a steel mill. I frequently saw him carry a silver metal lunch bucket, a heavy looking, no-nonsense food carrier. Because real steel men didn't tote lunches in paper sacks.

His lunch bucket was so impressive, it influenced my earliest career goal. I wanted a serious lunch pail to bring to my steel mill job. Now this might seem to be a modest goal, but at that time, for me, it was a reach-out.

Lollar

Jack Lollar and I were Little League Baseball teammates. His dad was our coach. Like myself, Jack wasn't much of a player. But his dad was a terrific coach. Mr. Lollar had played professionally and he structured our practices like the pros.

He taught us proper defensive positions with runners on base, base coverage responsibility, backup positions, cutoffs and relays on balls hit to the outfield. We played pepper, learned how to bunt, hit & run, plate discipline, choking up on the bat, going to the opposite field.

One of Mr. Lollar's teaching lessons was most memorable. During a game I had allowed a slow rolling grounder to go through my legs. It was a pathetic error. Between innings, Mr. Lollar sat down next to me and told me to shake it off and to always keep my dobber up.

It was helpful advice. When I ran out to my position, I was totally committed to an upper dobber. No way was that dobber going down. Except even though I knew I must have a dobber, I didn't know what or where my dobber was.

Russo

My initial weekly collection greeting was Paperboy, *Daily Herald Tribune Times Journal* 40 cents. But I soon found this unnecessarily formal and lengthy. I figured out that my customers had figured out why I stood at their door. And my intro was shortened to Paperboy, 40 cents. Then just Paperboy. And ultimately, I could just knock and say nothing.

The streamlined greeting was more efficient. But collection efficiency was really determined by who answered the door. If it was a kid, it was a minimum two-step process. They had no money. Adult women rarely had money on their person, but they knew where the cash was stashed. The collecting efficiency sweet spot were adult men. They usually toted money with them.

But easily the slowest customer payment stop was the Russo's. They were a robust sized clan, so large I never got an accurate count. And my door knock would unleash a herd of kids swarming to their front door. It was scary.

My six plus years visit would bring the kids efficiently to the door but the gang reacted to my weekly collection as a new and unexpected event. Paperboy? Who? What? Why? Need money? Hmmm, what to do? Didn't see this coming.

Baranowski

Jack and Mary Baranowski were seriously large people. Their bigness was not a big deal to me until one day it grew into a kinda big deal.

Ignoring the rule to never toss the paper, I had gotten pretty good at backhanded, frisbee style paper tosses. But this day my toss toward the Baranowski stoop got away from me. Perhaps I didn't get it on the proper takeaway plane or failed to make a full body turn or maybe I held on too long before the release. Anyway, the rubber banded tabloid flew from my sidewalk position onto the edge of the Baranowski roof gutter. It dangled there like a participle.

Hoping it would eventually drop, I moved on. But the next day I saw Mr. Baranowski standing on the sidewalk in front of his house. Suspecting he might want to discuss the gutter roof paper, I launched with hey, Mr. B., was that a windy day yesterday or what?

He ignored my greeting and said his paper was on his roof yesterday. I gave him my best theatrical stunned and confused look. It was a decent portrayal of not following where he was going with this. He ignored my stunned and confused look and said because he was a large man, he needed his newspaper near his front door, so he didn't have to look for it. Or walk far to retrieve it or climb his ladder to his roof, where he found yesterday's paper.

My reaction was naturally defensive. His assumption I was the cause of his displaced paper was presumptuous. In addition to wind being a potential cause, the neighborhood was hardly trustworthy. There were an endless number of potential reasons for a roofed paper. But something about Mr. B's mood caused me to keep this as thought bubble babble.

Mr. B. concluded our discussion with a verbal dagger. He said this never happened with Bob, which seemed to me to be over the roof unnecessary for him to state the obvious.

O'Gara

My paper route collection money was easily managed. It went into my shoulder-strapped cloth bag, zipped shut. But with my new wealth, I needed a personal money management system.

Mr. O'Gara retrieved coins from an oval-shaped plastic slitted container. I thought it was cool. So, I bought a Mr. O'Gara look alike. Unfortunately, it came without instructions and surprisingly, the seemingly simple receptacle was intricate.

When new, the plastic container was quite rigid. To open the slit, finger pressure was applied to the tiny holes at each end. This required not just finger strength but also eye-hand coordination. And unlike Mr. O'Gara's effortless, veteran manipulation, I struggled to master the aerodynamic physics of the slit system.

There were some other inherent technical flaws with the slit. It had limited capacity. Best suited for thin dimes. But the dimes would get wedged in the crevices. And when the rigidity of the hard plastic softened, the slit would remain ajar and dimes would slip out.

My struggles with the slit system were finally resolved by what became a frequent approach to many of my challenges. I decided to quit the slit.

Madigan

Mr. Madigan was an elected politician. He held a county office, I think.

Collecting one evening, I asked Mr. Madigan if he liked being a politician. Well Tommy, he began, I'll have to think about that. I might put that on my back burner and probably, after more consideration, get back to you later. But I'm curious. Why do you ask?

I told him I thought I might someday want to be a politician.

OK, well then, he continued, some might think, but could be mistaken, and I can't speak for everyone, keeping your options open might be a smart move. There are times when avoiding or delaying a career choice is the prudent approach. A choice or a stance never taken can rarely be wrong or bad. And seldom creates regret. So, it's wise to hedge your bets by covering all bases; advisable to avoid commitments that might back you into a career decision corner.

He went on by saying without further thought, I hesitate to offer a firm point of view. My reluctance is because I'm currently on the fence. But that's not my final word.

What I'm kind of saying is I would not recommend but wouldn't rule out recommending a political career. So, I couldn't really say yes or say no.

Would you say maybe, I asked? I might, he said.

Borio

I had been called names, but nothing ever stuck. Like a nickname. I don't remember if I thought this was good, bad, or if I ever thought about it.

Most customers greeted me or referred to me generically as the paperboy or if specific, Tom or Tommy. But Mr. Borio never called me paperboy, Tom, or Tommy. But he did greet me with a variety of names.

Hey, there's the big guy; the big kid; the big fella; the big shooter. Or, hiya tiger, howsitgoin slugger? Howyadoin kiddo? Hangin in there buddy? You doin OK pal? What's new cowboy?

I never thought of myself as a big guy, kid, fella, or shooter. Never felt like a tiger, slugger, kiddo, buddy, pal, cowboy. And I doubt he thought I was a big guy, kid, fella, shooter, tiger, slugger, kiddo, buddy, pal, cowboy. I think he probably called me big guy, kid, fella, tiger, slugger, kiddo, buddy, pal, cowboy because he just couldn't remember my name.

Murphy

Although I didn't know why, I had heard the Irish were lucky. And that was true with my Irish friend, Mickey Murphy. He was quite lucky.

Among the several examples of Mickey's luck, I'll only share one. Mickey didn't have a belly button. I never knew nor asked how it became missing. And Mickey never tried to borrow one of ours.

And why would he? When all the girls thought his missing belly button was just so cute. For reasons only girls could explain. They begged Mick to flash his flabby tummy belly, sans button.

God this was annoying. And thoroughly unfair. It was hard enough to impress girls. Challenging to get their attention. Then Mickey has this cute no belly button thing going. Not just going. Gone. How do you compete with that? Lucky Irish jerk.

Crow

Mr. & Mrs. Crow and their son George were Indians. Someone had said they were feathered, not dotted. I didn't understand the meaning of the distinction.

Early in my paperboy career George, a couple years older than myself, told me his people had discovered America. Wow, you're related to Columbus? No, he said. Columbus didn't discover America. My people did.

Now I knew his parents were old, but how old were they? Anyway, I did recall wondering how Columbus discovered this place when there were already some people here. But at the time of this thinking, there were so many mysteries getting tossed at me in school—a guy walking on water, ascending into the sky—some mysteries got shoved into the back seat.

Not sure his parents discovered America, but they might have discovered big garages. Because the Crows had the largest garage in the neighborhood. It was a detached monstrosity that swallowed the entire backyard. This was no tepee. This was a Taj Mahal.

Within the Mahal was a weightlifter's shrine. A collection of dead weights to make Arnold Schwarzenegger drool. George was so ripped he must have been born with muscles and then added more to that birth batch.

I asked George why he worked so hard working out. He told me he was considering seceding from the neighborhood to create his own sovereign neighborhood. He thought that might create some pushback so he was bulking up for a potential fight.

That made perfect sense to me and sounded cool and exciting. I asked how can I help?

Sullivan

It was common for me to observe next-door neighbors hanging out together. They generally gathered on front stoops. I suppose the gatherings occurred because they were right next door.

Sammy Sullivan, a little older than me, was always next door at the Ryans. So frequently I initially thought he was a Ryan family member, assuming his name was Sammy Ryan. I had minimal interactions with just Sammy without his next-door buddy, Teddy Ryan.

Ryan

Teddy Ryan and Sammy Sullivan were partners. Individually they seemed like decent guys, but as a duo their duet presence gave me an intuitive feeling of discomfort. This intuition turned out to be accurate one day early in my paper route employment.

Delivering the Ryan paper, they were sitting on Teddy's front stoop. I thought I heard a dog but couldn't see it. Foolishly, in retrospect, I asked Teddy if he had a dog. His response was briefly delayed as he, for some reason, glanced at Sammy before saying you haven't met Puppy? Well, come on, follow me. He's in the backyard.

Something told me not to go. But my inner caution voice was vetoed by my inner wimp voice and I followed them.

Backyards were generally un-notable spaces. But the Ryan backyard was notable for its notableness. Their small plot of barren rock-hard dirt was void of grass or anything green; even the weeds had moved out. This hidden rear topography suffered from some severe neglect. But it quickly became apparent Puppy had made a significant contribution.

Puppy was a large scrawny mongrel, tethered to a chain with elephant retention strength and car towing capability. The chain was secured to a steel stake to make Dracula nervous, embedded into concrete-like dirt footings.

My reluctance omen was insightful. Because Teddy says to Sammy, hey, let's feed Tommy to Puppy. And they started to drag me against my feeble resistance toward this nasty animal. Puppy, likely sensing the poignant fear wafting off me, went ballistic; spittle spraying, angry vocal renderings, lunging with the chain taut, focused, committed. Not sure when his last meal was.

Desperate, I actually began to pray that God would intervene and reinforce *Puppy's* containment system to prevent me from becoming his snack.

Laughing hysterically, Teddy and Sammy finally let me go. Teddy said just kiddin' Tommy; we wouldn't let Puppy eat you. As my heart tried to recalibrate, Sammy said I gotta go. He said that in such a bored, ho-hum manner, the only thing missing was his yawn. It was as if what had just happened didn't happen.

Andy Warhol said everyone would have 15 minutes of fame. I'm pleased mine wasn't accomplished as the first paperboy to die as a dog dinner entree.

Fortunato

Mark Fortunato and I were in the same Cub Scout den. Our meetings were held at his house because his mom was our den mother. Mrs. Fortunato was a perfect den matriarch to lead young cubs—supportive, encouraging, patient. Consistently in a pleasant mood.

My cub scout tenure was brief. I quit and I wish I could say it was because I got the paper route. But my scout quit was to escape the business segment of the meetings. Those activities frequently involved some sort of building project, most required glue. Glue and I never stuck. I struggled to apply the correct dab amount and placement onto popsicle sticks and the like.

And with my quit, Mrs. Fortunato also quit. She quit being my den mother but she remained my paper customer mother.

Ricci

In fifth grade, I became closer to Patti Ricci. The class seating chart had Patti's desk positioned directly in front of me. And then the Russians brought me even closer.

The Russians were a Cold War foe with warm nuclear capability, deemed a serious U.S. threat. So, at school we prepared for their potential sneak attack. Our primary death-avoiding maneuver was to crawl under our school desk and hide. Even our nun teacher crawled under her desk. But her desk wasn't the same. Her desk was bigger. But she was also bigger. So maybe it was the same.

Anyway, there was little for me to do sub-desk except peek at Patti's underpants. This may sound like I was a creepy paperboy panty peeker, but I wasn't the only one. I mean yeah, I was the only paperboy. But to my knowledge, Patti was the only flagrant panty poser. So, what was I to do? Close my eyes and risk missing the Russian missiles?

And it wasn't even a sexual thing. At the time. And by the time it might have been, we stopped desk hiding. The Russians changed their minds about discovering Cuba. They took their missiles and went home.

Christopherson

Mr. Christopherson was the Christopherson paper payer. One time when I was told he was in the garage, I found him stacking cardboard boxes. The boxes contained liquor bottles. Thus, I surmised he was a liquor salesman. He had an impressive stash of spirits.

Not long after that, during my collection rounds one evening, I ran into Sammy Sullivan and Teddy Ryan. Teddy was carrying a paper sack. With a pride, borderline brag, Teddy opened the bag and produced a bottle of liquor. With even more pride and brag, he said he had stolen it from the Christopherson garage.

Teddy and Sammy told me they had decided to start a drinking club and asked me if I wanted to join.

I think I was about twelve years old, the usual time when boys leave the Age of Innocence and enter the Age of Male Mental Fog; i.e., stupid thinking. I had already sampled church wine and thought maybe I should expand my alcohol exploration. So I accepted their kind invitation. And the other reason I agreed to join was a concern my decline might prompt another *Puppy* feeding.

We walked the short distance to the alley behind the church where all kids' illicit clubs and activities convened because the church had no rear windows. A bottle of stolen blackberry brandy emerged from its hidden hiding place and was passed around. My initial brandy imbibe was a brief interior visit. One sip generated my immediate regurgitation. That generated loud guffaws from my club peers.

Our disturbance must have been the cause of the church back door flying open where Father George loomed and then boomed "you kids get the hell out of here." I've never been so glad to see a priest. I immediately took off and lost Teddy and Sammy, but I heard them behind me. It sounded like maybe running and blackberry brandy didn't play well together.

O'Flannery

Among the many distractions that negatively impacted the quality of my customer service, Billy O'Flannery was a frequent cause. When I collected from the O'Flannery's, rather than taking care of business and moving on, I began to hang out with Billy.

Which was a little surprising. Even though we were the same age, he was a brainiac and myself less so. Our bond was built playing Billy's two war battle board games; one was a world war, the other U.S. Civil war. Both had miniature soldiers, canons, and war ships, color coded to designate the conflicting armies.

Our wars were lengthy, time-consuming battles. Time borrowed from my collecting duties. Although I put up a good fight, Billy always won. Regardless if he commanded the allies or axis powers, or the north or south armies. He was lucky. An incredible string of luck, luckily deploying his military resources to geographical battle advantage.

I've long ago lost track of Billy, but my hope is he brought his lucky deployment strategies to the U.S. military.

Nielson

The Nielson household had no Mr. Nielson, nor any mini-Nielson's, just Mrs. Nielson. Her house was located within what I considered to be the upscale, hoity but not quite toity portion of my paper route. It consisted of two houses, with Mrs. Nielson the pillar or anchor.

Now for some reason, Mrs. N. always made me feel like I needed a bath. Maybe because I did. Everything about Mrs. Nielson seemed formal to me. She spoke formally, was always formally dressed, perfectly manicured. And not just her person, not just her house, but also her yard. Her flowers, lawn and hedges were paper route comparative trophies. And her trophies were a source of intermittent conflict between us.

From day one, she made it explicitly clear I was never to cut across her lawn or forge through her hedges. Sidewalks, she explained, were originally invented for proper paperboy use.

I heeded her wish. Usually. Except when I was working on a new paper delivery land speed record—thirty-seven minutes; a single trip Monday edition so thin I could put all of the papers into the two cloth bags, alternately strapped over both shoulders. In contrast, the Sunday paper was so thick, it took me three trips back to the house to reload.

Anyway, Mrs. Nielson always caught me. She must have had a hidden speed trap; maybe a radar system. And when I was pulled over, Mrs. N. gave me an "I'm disappointed in you" speeding ticket. This was usually accompanied by a reminder that Bob had a perfect compliance record.

Before moving on, I'm concerned I have portrayed Mrs. Nielson in a less than flattering manner. Not so. I think she may have seen me as a boy needing help. Someone under her tutelage that might be sculpted into an acceptable human hedge. Her failure was not her fault.

Warsky

Mrs. Nielson was no hedgehog. She shared her hedges with the Warsky's who also shared her protective yard and hedge perspective. What was not shared was her "I'm disappointed in you" response when I was caught cutting through their abutted side yard.

Mr. Warsky was the hedge police. A little less vigilant than Mrs. Nielson, but when I was nabbed, he invoked the customary adult man reprimand—a variation of the "knock it off kid." But Mr. Warsky's delivery of his bark didn't seem to me to have any threat of a bite.

This was proven when one time he emitted a sort of yip followed by a mumbled reference to my predecessor Bob. And Mrs. Warsky said "Ward, aren't you being a little hard on the paperboy?" Momentarily I felt I had stepped into a *Leave it to Beaver* TV episode. Mr. Warsky apologized to me. Then I said "well I hope you've learned a lesson, old man."

I didn't say that. I just thought of that now. But I wish I had said it because that would have been funny.

Koziel

The Koziel family had many kids. Not so unusual. And they were a friendly and seemingly happy group. Again, not too rare. But what was distinct was Mr. Koziel's nearly constant smile, a little uncommon for the adult men and dads on my paper route.

He wasn't necessarily an outgoing guy. He wasn't continuously laughing. I never heard him whistling or humming. He just had this contented, ever-present grin.

Mr. Koziel was a butcher at a local grocery store. My knowledge of butchering was limited. But I assumed his job likely required cutting up animals. An occupation that seemed to me to be at odds with serial smiling.

This conundrum was only solved recently. I stumbled onto some research by Bain & Associates, a consulting think tank. Their study found that of all employee's, grocery employees were identified as the most sexually active and satisfied. And among grocery personnel, the meat department housed the most sexually engaged and pleased.

Had I known this earlier in life, my working career may have taken a different path.

Bukowski

Someone once said that dogs are man's best friend. Perhaps, but my paper route experience proved dogs were not a paperboy's best friend. I should qualify that by stating some dogs were OK. Dogs that didn't attack, bite, jump, or slobber on me. In other words, dogs restrained by leashes and chains.

The Bukowskis told me they were getting a watchdog. And they wanted me to befriend it as a watchpup before it became a watchdog and did its watchdog thing on me. I don't know why, but not surprisingly, I ignored their advice.

Ogden Nash, a long-ago humorous poet, said a door is what a dog is always on the wrong side of. For me, the Bukowski dog was always on the right side of their door. Because every day of my visits the dog threw a full body slam into that door with a blood curdling dog-speak *you're dead meat if I get to you.*

One afternoon the dog pummeled the door as usual. But the door didn't hold. As I headed toward the next house, the watchdog busted through, making a dogline version of a beeline after me. Just before I died, watchdog managed to trip over a gutter downspout, his growl turned to yips, momentarily halting his meal chase.

Luckily, Mr. Bukowski had immediately given chase and while he delivered first responder dog aid, he accusingly asked if I would stop beating up on his pet. I apologized and told him I had anger issues that I was working on. I then suggested re-enforcing his front door for the dog's protection.

Now I have shared this story many times. And veteran dog owners have told me a dog would never trip over a downspout. I wouldn't know but what I do know is that dog did. And my guess is there has never been a dog with that much focus that he just ignored the obstruction.

Chang

Mr. Frank Chang, a middle-aged bachelor, was a small man with a large personality. He was outgoing, loud, sassy, and funny. And kind.

Mr. Chang was the owner of Chang's Chinese takeout, located next door to Andy's Tavern. And it was at Andy's, not his house or restaurant, where I usually collected from him. He was frequently playing high stakes gin, the cash discreetly hidden beneath a huge black hard plastic ashtray on a bar room table.

Because of Mr. Chang, it was both more fun and profitable collecting at Andy's. Upon my entry, Mr. Chang would shout "All right everybody, get your money out and pay Tommy for the paper." (Even some non-customers would also pay me, even after I told them they weren't my customers.) "And Frankie, get Tommy a beer. On cue, Frankie said he's trying to quit. OK, get him a Coke.

Columbo

Mr. & Mrs. Columbo had three daughters. Brenda, the youngest, was a grade ahead of me. And Brenda was my first physically romantic partner. It was a brief affair—a one day fling. Actually, and more accurately, maybe about twelve minutes. Whatever. That's not important. What's important is how we maximized those twelve minutes.

Delivering her paper late one afternoon, our tryst began when Brenda laughed at something I said. Could it get any better than that? Yes. Brenda said nobody was home. Did I want to come in and play?

When our social conversation lagged, Brenda stepped up her hostess game. She asked if I wanted to kiss her. Well, I thought that maybe I did. Because I had never kissed a girl, and I was nearing my twelfth birthday.

Seated cross-legged on her carpeted front room floor, I leaned forward, lips puckered, eyes closed, and sought her mouth. But my balance was a little unbalanced and I delivered a glancing blow to the bottom of her right ear lobe. She told me to scoot closer. It was helpful advice. The re-kiss made some contact with the side of her nose. Brenda suggested I open my eyes. After assurance that it was allowable, my eye opening third effort made a lip stick.

We both agreed that it was fun and with our kissing business concluded, I left to return to my news business. And I mentally broke down the game film on our lip match. Because losing my kiss virginity warranted scrutiny.

I must admit I was a little disappointed. Shouldn't a first kiss be, I don't know, world rocking? Mine wasn't. Was this a case of unrealistic expectations? Maybe a result of my lack of a kiss goal? And I wondered how Brenda felt. She said it was fun, but was that just lip service?

We never improved upon that inaugural smooch. It was our final kiss—a one and done. Our romantic fire flickered, then went out. It would be about two more years before I would be able to deploy the skill that Brenda had so graciously taught me.

CUSTOMER COLLECTIONS

I've provided some clues into my thinking, but here is a little more insight. My young brain evolved and expanded during my collection duties.

The rule was to collect customer payment strictly on Monday and Tuesday. But soon, my collecting bled into Wednesday, then Thursday, and ultimately, also Friday.

This collection time inflation had several causes. Sports events and distractions playing with friends were the most frequent. But another reason for the extension was rather than collect, sometimes I would just wander through the neighborhood. During those nomadic wanders, I wondered. Thought about stuff. This wasn't daydreaming. That was a school activity. This was nightdreaming into deep analytical thought.

These wandered wonderings were primarily a warm weather activity. Winter disrupted the depth of my musings. My hooded jacket obscured my peripheral vision, the wind diluted my hearing and the early darkness and snow required my attention to traverse the inconsistent walking surfaces. This physical focus was discordant with the mental attention needed to get into my deepest layer thought zones.

But interestingly, my best analysis actually happened during winter. At the neighborhood coin laundromat, located next to Chang's Chinese take-out, two doors from Andy's Tavern. After collecting at Andy's, where several customers were always present, the laundromat became my warm sacred space to scan and surf my mental collage of topics.

The laundry environment stimulated thought provocation. The cleansing of clothing seemed to induce my mental cleansing. The wash cycle washed away my brain cobwebs. And as clothes tumbled around in their drying battles, my creative thoughts tumbled forth. The aroma of fresh laundry freshened my mind. It became my epistemological development lab.

Hmm. I'm pretty pleased with the above metaphorical blah blah. But what remains unsaid is what did I think about?

Well, as a professional paperboy, it's logical that I focused upon how to improve the quality of my paper service. How I might truly delight my customers. But that not only never happened, it never even occurred to me to happen.

But I did think about adults. Because my paper route expanded my adult interaction universe. And with that came more opportunity for conflicts between their needs and mine and their expectations and my ability to meet those expectations.

When my laziness was mixed with a leisure focus and a dash of looking at rules as general guidelines, those recipe ingredients didn't cook an appealing meal to many older pallets. And some of them called me out for my behavior, because that was their job. Their assessment had a remarkable track record for accuracy and validity, leaving me little wiggle room to disagree. I suppose I should have thought about ways to stay out of their doghouses or, minimally, how to get out of those residences.

What else did I think about? You know, the usual deep topics for a young paperboy: what was a dobber and where was mine? Why did I get a C when I thought I had a C+ locked in? How do I take my marble game to the next level? Where do I find a Mickey Mantle baseball card? Can I improve my 37-minute paper delivery speed record? Dogs and other stuff.

As I think about what I might have thought about, maybe what I thought about is less important than just actually thinking. But then at about age thirteen, my analysis became more meaningful. I started to focus and think almost exclusively about girls. Pretty much non-stop. And I shifted from trying to understand adult thinking to try to understand girls thinking.

Trying to understand girls was much harder than adults. Way harder. I'm talking about a real challenge. Difficult. Befuddling. Arduous. Tough. Am I clear? Got it?

TAVERN TRAIL

Ladd

Mr. Ladd lived in the only two-story house on my paper route. Which made sense. Because Mr. Ladd was seven feet tall. Neighborhood kids called him "The Ladder."

My very first encounter with Mr. Ladd was memorable. Because he told me he had never played basketball. This information was interesting for two reasons. One, he didn't answer my posed question, he just volunteered this. That was remarkable. How did he know I was wondering? But more amazing was that he never did play the sport where his height would be so advantageous.

But his height did bring up another question. Did he buy the house because it was tall? Or was it originally short and he grew it to accommodate his tallness? I never posed that question either, I just assumed it was the latter.

Siminski

The Siminski's usual response to my collecting door knock was "Johnny's got it."

Johnny was the Siminski door man, designated greeter, and I suppose, security guy. A little remarkable given Johnny was about three feet tall. He was a notable vertical contrast to his next door neighbor Mr. Ladd. I suppose this might be an example of the diversity of my paper customers, but it was more likely a temporary result of Johnny being only five years old.

Anyway, Johnny and I fell into an interactive door routine. I would tell Johnny to go get someone taller. Johnny, a smart kid, said you're taller. You are correct. But go get someone taller from your family. Aren't you my brother? In his defense, it was a large family. No, I'm not your brother. I'm the paperboy. And I need money. His reply was who doesn't?

He was not only a short smart kid, but he was also a short smart-ass kid.

Houlihan

Joey Houlihan and I were buddies. Our buds grew because we were both sports junkies—Joey was the one with athletic talent. But his real skill was linguistics. Specifically, his belching renditions. Or was it burping? Not sure if there's a difference, but there probably is because why else would there be two different words?

Anyway, before I elaborate on Joey's art form, let me tip my verbal hat to God's sense of humor. If not hilarity, what other purpose did human noises serve? Loud farts, for example, are hilarious, particularly in grade school classrooms and during church services. Some nasal noises can be screamers—a spontaneous tuba/goose honking sneeze explosion can be a side splitter. And of course, burps and belches.

Now a lot of guys could and would belch and burp, but Joey was distinctive for two reasons. One was his sustainability. Ignoring the limitations and physics of human air capacity, he could speak belch/burp sentences. And secondly, his renderings covered the entire vocal spectrum—soprano through bass. As I reflect upon Joey's unique utterances, I wonder if he may have had an early influence on Peter Frampton.

Like most of the guys, I was envious of Joey's skill. My feeble efforts were never in his league, and so, like many of my activities, I gave up trying. Or maybe I grew up. But that's less likely, because males continue to laugh at human noises until roughly age fifty-eight. Females lose appreciation for this form of humor at about six years of age.

Beach

Mr. & Mrs. Beach were childless. Mr. Beach was a breakfast cook at a small greasy spoon. His workday began early and ended early, which allowed him to relax by mid-afternoon. On some warm summer days, he and Mrs. Beach lay on recliners, drinking beer in their yard.

Mr. Beach had an incredible stomach. This detail is hardly noteworthy because at that time, men's stomach protrusions were common, apparently in vogue then and hasn't entirely gone out of style currently. But Mr. Beach's gut was not your generic tummy extension. It wasn't what Mom would kindly describe as fleshy. His flesh didn't jiggle from loose skin, it was totally taut, as if he had swallowed an overinflated beach ball.

It was during these warm day lounging sessions that I got to know him. He had been a cook in the army. After his military duty, without any previous experience, he was hired as a waiter at an upscale restaurant. And he shared with me some humorous yarns about his inexperience during that stint in his culinary career.

Like his champagne cork launch that took down part of a chandelier. Or his inaugural table-side flaming Chateaubriand preparation—his overly aggressive application of the flambé fire starter spit out some sparks onto the carpeted floor, the smoldering smoke engulfed and emptied the restaurant.

One hot summer night, a droplet of his forehead sweat flopped into a diner's soup. And then there was the time when a female patron accepted his offer to crack and remove crab from the shell. In the process, a slippery morsel flew up and then down the inside of her dress top. He instinctively reached down, and brought the aquatic dead creature up, but her dress top came partially down, and awkwardness entirely went up.

Here's my favorite. While serving sour cream from his Lazy Susan to a baked potato, enroute to the spud, a dollop plopped off the ladle and nestled into the back of a woman's flipped hair do. She was unaware because her coif was hair sprayed stiff enough to support a brick. He decided to ignore it, in hopes her later discovery wouldn't suspect he was the donor.

The sour cream incident concluded his fancy restaurant waiter tenure. After his dismissal, from the high end eatery, he decided to do a 180 and go low brow. Hence, his career move to the grill at the greasy spoon.

While I cracked up at these stories and Mr. Beach broadly smiled, for some reason Mrs. Beach was strangely silent. I wondered why.

Ciceroni

Lenny Ciceroni was a neighborhood alpha male. Alphas were older boys, usually decent athletes, skilled trash talkers, with a tough guy reputation. An alpha reign was short. They were young enough to still hang out with younger kids but not old enough to stop caring and move on.

The alpha influence on younger boys was their insights. They knew stuff that wasn't common knowledge and dispensed their information to the male youth who appreciated the news and accepted it with little, if any, pushback.

One summer afternoon following a pick-up baseball game, Lenny revealed how babies were made. The initial silence from our less worldly group inferred this was likely true. There were a couple of ignorant-disguising mumbled grunts to suggest like who doesn't know that.

Well, I certainly didn't know that. My head hung down; eyes fixated on the dirt beneath my feet as I tried to process this shocking news. My ten-year-old brain grappled with the mental projection of Mom and Dad. They did this? I don't think so. Can't be. No way.

At that moment, all my energy was focused on trying to purge this out of my head and then erase it permanently.

Petronelli

My lack of artistic skills was the likely driver of my art curiosity. But my interest in art was less about actual works of art, and more about the creative creators. And perhaps a little less about their talent than their oddities. Artists just struck me as a little odd and odd had an odd appeal. Like Gino Petronelli.

Gino, the eldest of the large Petronelli family, was a thin kid with a tattoo near his skinny bicep. From my brief skin scan it looked like an ink smudge. Or an epidermal Rorschach test. I couldn't really decipher what it depicted. But that didn't dilute my admiration for his flesh art.

When I expressed my kudos, he told me he had tatted it himself. And I suppose because of my interest, Gino invited me into his house and into the bedroom he shared with his brothers. Tacked upon the walls were several paper pen and pencil drawings in various sizes but similar renderings. The creations reminded me of early cave dweller art.

Thankfully, he answered my silent question telling me they were wolves. He then put his arm art next to his wall art and told me it was the same wolf. He further explained that he was an impressionist with a focus on the still-life wolf niche, ala fruit still-life.

The purpose, he continued, for his arm tattoo was to serve as a walking billboard, his initial marketing strategy to generate interest in his art stuff. An obviously effective strategy, as it got me into his gallery. I felt privileged to be invited to Gino's one-man showing and remain vigilant for news of Gino's discovery and presence upon the global art world stage.

Sarello

Most of my customers were mostly nice. But the exception was Tony Sarello.

For whatever reason, he managed to rub me the wrong way. Maybe because he worked at a rubber factory, and the rubber rubbed off onto me. His know-it-all personality was unpleasant. As was his incessant need to tease me. I think he thought it was great fun. I humored him with smiles but secretly found his humor humorless.

Now I don't want to make this a big deal. I don't have a bunch of specific examples to share. But I do have one. One day in 1965, age 14, just shy of 15, he told me in a few years I would go to Vietnam where I would get my ass shot.

What? Did he think he was a fortune teller? His forecast so annoyed me that just to prove him wrong, I made a self-promise to avoid Vietnam. But one challenge to my avoidance commitment was I didn't know where Vietnam was, a small but formidable obstacle for avoidance.

Initially I assumed Vietnam was a dangerous, nasty neighborhood. When I later found out where it was, I was relieved to learn at least one ocean was between me and there, eliminating me from unwittingly wandering into it.

McKeon

Mr. & Mrs. McKeon had four young, pretty daughters. When Mr. McKeon paid me for the paper bill, he was always friendly. I'm not sure why, but he seemed to like me. Maybe I was the boy he never had?

Mr. McKeon had a boss type job at the main post office. One evening, when I was sixteen, deep into my paperboy career, he asked me what my future plans were. I said I would probably be done collecting about 8:30 PM. He clarified, what were my plans after high school?

At that point, I had no plans, but thought I should make something up. So I told him I might go to college. He said if I did, come see him and maybe he could help. A couple years later, I did go to college and I did go see Mr. McKeon. And he helped me get a part time job at the post office under a federal program for students.

I was a little surprised that Mr. McKeon would entrust me to deliver the U.S. Mail—my paperboy delivery wasn't always reliable. But it turned out my job didn't entail delivery—my duties were to sort the long from the short envelopes for postage meter metering's. And equally important, sort the zip codes for the mail carriers.

Anyway, I really appreciated Mr. McKeon's help. And to show my appreciation, I worked hard at not getting fired.

Quinn

The teen years were a challenge. Confidence was shaky and then acne showed up.

Tom Quinn was my age and a good friend. Unfortunately, Tom's acne was the worst. His entire face broke out in nasty white pus-filled pimples. And this malady extended onto his neck, arms, and shoulders. He was a mess.

I felt sorry for Tom. Initially. But my empathy waned when word got out that all the girl's thought Tom was just the cutest, hottest boy on earth. That kind of information traveled rapidly.

Girls were so strange. Confusing, mysterious enigmas. It forever surprised me who they decided to worship or adore. Their choices frequently left me thinking really? Anyway, Tom and I remained friends. But my concern for his skin condition left and was replaced by my jealousy. He was just a lucky guy to have that mess.

Fracaro

My pal Jim Fracaro was called Butch, a nickname that implied a tough guy. And Butch was a tough kid, but a quiet, nice-guy tough. He wasn't a bully. But he was a marble champ.

Kid games had a lifespan—Mumblypeg died before my birth, kick-the-can had been kicked down the street, red-light green-light, hide-and-go-seek, and red rover were vague memories from early in my youth.

Tiddlywinks was barely hanging on. And Marbles was on life support, nearing end of life. Butch seemed to single handedly keep Marbles alive, hosting games in his backyard.

Within the kid game world, Marbles was unique. The results of the game had financial consequences. Marble wealth grew or shrank based upon a win or loss which was impacted by skill rather than luck.

Success in Marbles required shooting a sphere out of the crevice between thumb and pointer finger. With accuracy, sufficient gusto, and spin to stop the shooting spheroid within a dirt-drawn circle while knocking any marbles outside the circle which were kept.

Butch was a great Marbles player. I was bad. And so I consistently lost marbles to Butch and anyone else who played. My marble supply within my oval cardboard Quaker Oats box continued to shrink. Leaving me with three potential remedies—improve my skill, buy more marbles, or quit. My prudent decision was to quit.

Maranowski

When I collected for the paper in the early evening, Jimmy Maranowski paid me. He was a single child two years my junior. I felt sorry for Jimmy. Because he always came to the door in his pajamas.

Door answering clothing wasn't memorable or remarkable. There was the occasional robed door appearance, but nobody's garb really grabbed me. Only the girls in my family wore pajamas—the boys slept in our underwear. So, when Jimmy appeared pajama clad, I found it awkward.

I suppose his parents made him do it. Because they probably also had on their pajamas.

But maybe pajama wearing was more prevalent than I was aware. I never collected after 8:30 PM. Maybe customers waited until that paperboy door knock window shut, triggering a family announcement OK, all clear. Pajama time.

McMurphy

Patrick McMurphy was a retired priest. He no longer wore the cloth, but everyone still called him Father. He was a regular at Andy's Tavern, where I frequently collected from him.

It seemed odd to me that a priest lived in a neighborhood house. Then one day I finally asked him. And he invited me into his house for the first time.

That was the beginning of our transition from a business relationship into something more intimate. Now before I go there, don't you go there. Father McMurphy was not that kind of priest. But I suppose now is a good time to share my experience on this topic.

Recently, sporadic reports gained momentum. More and more stories of priests fondling boys. But as the stories proliferated, I remained silent. I was embarrassed. My scar never healed.

I was in the right place at the right time. Eight years of Catholic grammar school. Four years at a Catholic all-guys high school. Amid gangs of Jesuits and Carmelites. But nothing. Not a single fondle. In fact, not an ogle. No subtle body brushes. Nor momentary eye contact. No altered breathing in the confessional. Not a singular nuanced word.

In short, I was snubbed. I mean, I played sports. Hung out naked in the shower room. Was my young bare butt and tiny penis nothing to look at? Why did priests ignore me? And for the chrissake, I was an altar boy.

But never a priestly "hey, lookin' good in that cassock; red really works for you; nice candle handle; love your cruet work; mea culpa was particularly crisp this morning; wonderful genuflections, you been working out? Ever seen a naked man? Do you like gladiator movies?"

I don't know, my parents paid good money to send me to Catholic schools. Never stated but it was assumed there would be that little something extra; something that would suggest I wasn't necessarily special, but just a normal fondled boy.

Back to Father McMurphy's answer to my question, he told me his house was the original residence of Father Dave, St. Mary's founder. When the rectory was built, the parish decided to keep the house as part of Father Dave's retirement package and subsequently, his.

His candor was refreshing. He didn't pulpit spew mysterious gospel goop. He seemed like just an everyday guy. And he wasn't judgmental, surprisingly, given his career as a sinner judge. And so I became comfortable enough with Father M. to ask him another question that had been with me for a few years.

Probably somewhere about third grade, like most Catholic boys, I thought about becoming a priest, as did the girls becoming a nun. The Catholics knew how to get into a kid's head before the kid knew they had a head.

The nuns had the responsibility to answer big questions from little Catholic boys and girls. Like the question, how would I know if I wanted to be a priest or a nun? Their ambiguous response was God will let you know if you have a *calling*.

I wondered about the *call* and why I never got it. Or did I miss the *call*? Was it a collect *call* my parents didn't accept? Did the family not relay the message to me? I decided the *call* was unlikely. Although I was fine without a priest career invite, I remained curious how others got that dialup and accepted that heavenly reach out. So, I asked this real priest about his *call*.

Father M. told me he never got a *call*. He had always wanted to be Pope. Be the top guy. The priesthood was the first rung on the career ladder to Popedom. But a combination of bad luck and internal politics stalled his ladder climbing. He got permanently stuck at the priest step. Never moved up the organization chart.

That's sad, I said. Why didn't you just quit? Why would I? Being a priest hasn't been a bad ride. I have a nice pension. Live in this house for free. And I pick up some pocket change with a few baptisms and funerals side jobs.

I asked Father M. what he would have done if not a priest? He said sales. Really? Sure. Good money and I've got talent. Selling heaven and hell isn't easy, Tommy.

Longhini

The Longhini family had about eight kids. I liked large families because someone was likely home when I collected. They couldn't all fit into one car. And nobody had two cars.

Anyway, one evening after the Longhini's paid me, Steve, a year older than myself, caught up with me as I walked away. That was odd. People were generally done with me after I was done with them.

As we walked, he lit up a cigarette. He told me he needed a smoke. Made sense. As we walked down the sidewalk, we ran into Sammy Sullivan and Teddy Ryan who were also smoking. Steve suggested we start a smoking club. At age eleven, I thought it was time to take that next step into adulthood.

We went to the usual kid club meeting place—the alley behind the rear of the church. Steve laid out the club rules. We would meet weekly, taking turns bringing four cigarettes. I assumed they were to be stolen from our parents. The club meeting agenda would consist of smoking the cigarettes. Steve's detail was impressively comprehensive.

At that first meeting, I lit up, coughed up, and the church back door opened up. And there was Father George. The man ran a tight church. Before we asked who invited him, he asked "what are you goddamn kids doing here?" Apparently, the question was rhetorical because my club member peers had already taken off running. In support of club unity, I ran after them.

The smoking club disbanded. I don't remember why, but probably a combination of a lack of leadership and no suitable meeting space.

Poplowski

The Poplowski's were probably my wealthiest customer. This is based upon some sketchy analysis but I'll try to stretch that sketch.

There were three sources of paperboy profits. First, the difference between paper cost and customer price. Second, tips. Third, annual calendar sales.

The newspaper offered a new year's calendar for paperboy purchase. We could buy as many as we wanted for about ten cents apiece and then resell to customers for whatever price we chose. I thought fifteen or twenty cents was a good resale price point, a decent profitable markup. This was my thinking before my dad intervened.

He suggested I give them away. I thought, are you nuts? Did you not listen when I told you I paid for them? Why would I give them away?

He said the calendar would be my customer Christmas gift. Customers would then probably reciprocate. And likely exceed fifteen or twenty cents. Well, I decided to follow his suggestion. Not because I thought it was a good idea, but just to prove him wrong. Plus, I did think that Bob probably never gave his customers free calendars. And maybe customers would start to look at me with comparable favor.

Shockingly, Dad was correct. Even though that first year caught some customers off guard, I did way better than fifteen or twenty cents. And by the second year, everyone was on board. And my Christmas gifts from customers set new records. And not only cash gifts. Some home baked cookies appeared.

Which brings me back to the Poplowski's. Customer response to my calendar gift was my strongest insight into customer wealth. The Poplowski's gave me two dollars. A significant largesse. And bonafide wealth indicator if I ignored benevolence as a potential decision factor.

I thanked Dad for his brilliant calendar gift idea and tried it on him by giving him the twelve months. It didn't work. He stiffed me.

Sorrentino

Most adults were, from my youthful perspective, emotionally even keeled. Predictably consistent. For example, nuns and bus drivers were always crabby. Mr. Sorrentino was an inconsistent outlier.

There seemed to be two Mr. Sorrentino's. One was the friendly nice guy who greeted and paid me for the paper. The other Mr. Sorrentino was not so nice. *Mr. Not Nice* showed up at our 7th grade basketball games. He showed up because he was our coach.

One night our Catholic school team played a public-school team. At their public-school gym. We played a lot of road games because we didn't have a gym. Anyway, it was the perfect setup for an epoch Catholic vs. Pagan battle.

As a Catholic team, obviously God was on our side. But as I lined up for the opening tip, I glanced at the next guy. He was a foot taller. Muscle-bound. With a goatee. My first pubic hair was late arriving. God better bring his A-game I thought.

Just before halftime, I found myself the only defender against a large guy barreling toward our basket. I thought, not in my house buddy. But then I remembered it was his house. Not to be a rude guest, I politely and safely stepped aside. And admired his finish.

Within our halftime locker room, Coach *Not Nice* verbally ripped me for my gutless defense. Something about not doing my job. Although his verbal dress down I thought was well deserved, I also thought that was one lousy basket. We were down 44-8. Plus I thought, speaking of doing jobs, whose job was it to schedule our 7th grade team against this high school team?

Coach then delivered some yada, yada, pride spiel. Which surprisingly worked. We finished strong, 84-22 final score. The epoch battle missed both the epoch and battle part. The result had nothing to do with religion. They were good. We were bad. Not a victory formula. And God's off night didn't help.

Tortello

Beyond dogs, my paper route didn't have any wild animals. There were rumors of rats, but I never saw one. Saw a frog once. Later I learned it was a toad. Cats were common. But I had no issue with cats. We shared mutual fear, gave wide spatial berths, and unspoken respect.

But the Tortello's had a zoo. Both people and animals. A large family with many pets. Four dogs, three cats, a couple of snakes, an ant farm, a gerbil, goldfish, and a caged bird. It might have been a pelican, but my aviary knowledge was skimpy.

Except for the dogs, I thought the Tortello zoo was entirely contained within their house. But one afternoon, atop their rickety side yard fence, sat a pinkish, long-snouted, critter. Maybe it was an aardvark? I didn't know what an aardvark looked like, but I loved that word. And like thingamajig, hard to work into a sentence. Plus, I only got a fleeting look. The animal didn't fleet. I did.

Possibly it was a possum. If so, maybe it was on loan from another zoo. Perhaps it had migrated north from the southern U.S. to escape getting eaten. I'd heard possum was a delicacy in the south. I wondered if the Tortello's might be a part of a possum underground railroad?

Narakas

The Narakas family always invited me into their house when I collected. It was kind of them to do so, but I soon kinda wished they didn't. Because the Narakas house was a smellorium.

Many houses had some unique fragrance but the smell was usually subtle. The Narakas house odor was not only uniquely non-subtle, it was also mysterious. I couldn't identify the source. Maybe my nasal pipe had a technical flaw. Or perhaps my nostril intake system didn't have the bandwidth to process the smell volume. I was pretty sure it wasn't animal or human but I thought it might be food related.

I had a strong suspicion liver was a contributor. Catholics couldn't eat meat on Fridays, for what reason I never knew. Equally unknown was how liver, seemingly a meat product, somehow slipped through the meat ban crack. I suppose the liver people had a strong lobby at the Vatican.

So liver was one of the frequent Friday meat substitutes. Pre-cooked, it lay quivering like a bloody body organ freshly surgically extracted, not quite dead, but starting to rot—it really stunk or stank. I gag as I write. The cooked thing had the texture of a shoe.

Not to pick on liver, there were a couple of other weird Friday meat pinch hitters—creamed eggs on toast, creamed tuna on toast, creamed mushrooms on toast, and for variety, fried egg plant not on toast. I retain mental scar tissue from eating all of that disgusting stuff.

Anyway, my best guess was the Narakas house stench was a smell bomb combination of liver, creamed egg, fried egg plant, onions, garlic, tuna, sauerkraut, and cauliflower. And after preparation and consumption, the aroma just took up permanent residency.

I often wondered if they smelled what I smelled. Might their unique house smell have been a source of pride—an intentional signature statement? The mystery was never solved. They never asked me if their house stunk. And I never felt comfortable telling them it did or asking why. But I always felt comfortable quickly leaving.

Ivnik

Mr. Ivnik had two boys. Larry was a year younger than me, Matt a year older. On a summer afternoon, soon after I got the paper route, we played Hotbox in their yard—a great small space baseball game for three. Matt and I defended the bases. Larry, the base stealer, was in the "hotbox."

I backhanded one of Matt's wide throws, and my sweeping tag caught the sliding Larry on his arm. And Larry started to cry. That was surprising. My tag, unintentionally a tad hard, was not cry worthy.

Mr. Ivnik appeared and asked what happened. Larry said I smacked him. Mr. Ivnik said OK, either shake hands or we get the boxing gloves out. Boxing gloves?

Who owns boxing gloves? I was relieved when Larry said just forget it. I certainly had no desire to box.

Larry's crying continued to confuse me. Then I found out after this incident that shortly before I got the paper route and met Larry, his mom had died. And I wondered if maybe Larry cried a lot. I know I would have.

Torentino

Gary Torentino invited me to join his bowling team. I liked sports. Particularly team sports. And so I accepted his bowling team invitation.

But I soon figured out that Gary didn't have a team—teams require a sport, and bowling wasn't a sport. Now this is hard to pin down, but rolling a ball down a smooth surface to knock down stationary objects? I had to strike that from the sports genre. Do you disagree? Spare me.

I decided what Gary had was a club. And Gary was insightful that I was a good fit with the other chubby non-athletic club members. But my bowling club stint was short. Like many activities, I quit. Not because bowling wasn't a sport. It was a sport. And most likely the easiest of all sports. Which is why I had to quit. I was such a shitty bowler, it was embarrassing.

But my bowling experience was beneficial. Provided me insights into alleys and gutters. And I learned a new word, Kegling. Kegling has a nice sound. Aardvark-ish.

Rivera

Joey Rivera and I were buddies in grade school before I got the paper route. He was a quiet, humble, smart kid.

Except the nuns didn't know he was smart. He was from Mexico and his English language struggles hid his smartness.

Joey was the fastest runner in our class. He playfully laughed at my pathetic effort to beat him. I playfully and probably insensitively gave him shit about butchering our mother tongue.

When his family became one of my customers, I found out Joey had several sisters. At one point or another I think my heart beat a little quicker in the presence of nearly each one. And a different part of my body ached for Mrs. Rivera. Relax. I'll explain.

Mr. Rivera usually paid me for the paper. But when Mrs. Rivera paid me, she would frequently settle my aching tummy with some of her most incredible baked pastries. I can't remember if I mentioned that some of my customers had cash flow problems and would ask me to come back later in the week and sometimes, the following week. Mr. Rivera was the only customer I was tempted to ask if I could come back later, hoping Mrs. Rivera would pay me.

McSweeney

Father George delivered his annual mock mass to our sixth-grade class. At that time, most of the mass was conducted by the priest with his back to the congregation. And with his back turned, a spitball fight ensued. As usual, I was merely an innocent observer.

Until Larry McSweeney thwacked me with a wet globule. This was no tiny wad of moisturized paper. It felt like an entire roll of toilet paper had been submerged in holy water for days. It was a SCUD-*Soaked Crap Unidentified Debris.* SCUDs were banned by the Geneva Convention of International Spitball Rules.

This was an unprovoked attack. An assault so flagrant I could not turn my other cheek. Gandhi would have retaliated. I went into offensive mode. My wadded ammo loaded, I stood for maximum throwing leverage. Precisely in the middle of my cocked arm release, Father G. finished his "in nomine patrie, et filee, et spiritus sancti," and turned back toward us, and just as I let fly my wet missile, he bellowed my name so loud it must have startled pigeons for blocks.

And certainly startled our absent teacher, Sister O'Leary, back to the classroom door. Where she did the universal come here finger movement. I tried the confused look, glancing around me. But she didn't bite. Her pointer finger pointed directly at me.

I was marched down the hallway as she marched into a nasty verbal abuse assault. I was prepared to accept this tongue lashing until she said school was easy for me, but not for others. Like Larry McSweeney. I had selfishly robbed him of a learning opportunity.

What? Are you fucking kidding me? Where did she come up with this shit? Our one-way one-on-one concluded back at the classroom. Father G. had wrapped and gone. But she didn't allow me to return to my desk. I had to stand at the front as she asked the class to raise their hand if I had disrupted their learning.

As most of the boys checked their shoelace status, the girls' arms shot straight up. This was not surprising. Except that every girl's hand arose. Including Barb. Really? And JoAnne? No way. Mary? Say it ain't so. Sally, et tu?

I was expelled, pending trial at the convent. Where my nun prosecutor delivered compelling evidence of my education robbery. I was found guilty by my Mom jury, an open and shut case of rudeness. And sentenced to thirty days grounded. Sister O'Leary seemed pleased, unaware the sentence was essentially revoked by my paperboy duties.

Although I considered telling Larry that our nun thought he was stupid, I didn't. Because I didn't think he was a dummy, probably just a little more bored than most of us. Anyway, many years later, I was exonerated from stealing Larry's education. He became a professor at an Ivy League college, thankfully surviving my theft.

Adamik

I found all the dogs on my paper route to be collectively disturbing, in their own unique way. But the Adamik dog—Creeper, my name, not theirs—was the most uniquely disturbing.

Creeper had creepy eyes. They weren't partners; they were independent globes glowing with a strange red and yellow hue mixture hinting of a combination of embarrassment and jaundice. Creeper had a grooming problem that I suspected was the result of a bad grooming attitude.

The dog's body hair was a mixed mess of short mats with sporadic gelled spiked strands and intermittent alopecia bare spots. The tail hair looked as if someone had begun to eat an ear of corn, starting randomly in the middle, skipping some rows, then snarfing a few more.

Now maybe Creeper had an indecisive hairdresser or was working on an experimental style that hadn't come into vogue yet. But this was no bed head. This was bed body. I mean, we've all had bad hair days. Creeper had a bad hair life.

His teeth appeared to be taken from a dog cadaver and Elmer glued by a dentist with a nitrous addiction. The globule slime that emitted from its mouth would make Cujo jealous.

Anyway, all of that is cosmetic. Hardly noteworthy. What follows is the core issue.

Creeper was mysterious. I never saw the dog during the week. Only Saturday or Sunday mornings. And not every weekend. Was Creeper a college dog student? Returning home on some weekends for laundry or a good meal? Or was it an adult dog child unable to fully leave home. Or maybe the dog wasn't even family, but a moonlighting weekend guard dog.

Sometimes the dog would be on the front stoop of the Adamik house. Sometimes it would suddenly appear from some hidden space. And then creep silently, in a low crouch, with accelerating speed and lunge for the back of my leg.

If Creeper was hungry, understandable it would want a piece of me. But Creeper just wanted to fuck with me. Take a small nip; a nibble that never broke my skin. Like the dog was stealing a piece of candy rather than digging into a leg meal. Then creep away grinning. Really, I'm not making this up, Creeper grinned.

It always startled the holy shit out of me; creating a breath altering heart pounding spike, followed by my spontaneous variation of "God Dammit Dog! What's wrong with you? You have issues. Get some help."

CITY BUS

Every Saturday, after my morning paper delivery, I took the city bus downtown to the paper office to deliver the subscription money I had collected that week.

I remember feeling anxious on that first solo trip without Bob, my predecessor and mentor. One week short of ten years old, I carried a lot of cash in my collection bag. I decided to hide the cash bag beneath my jacket. And I also decided to sit on the bench seat directly behind the driver, assuming the driver would help me if anyone tried to steal my money.

My logic about the potential driver assistance, I discovered, was a little flawed, perhaps naïve. Because it became readily apparent that regardless of my seat selection, bus drivers couldn't be of any help to me if I needed their help.

In all my bus trips, I had never once witnessed a bus driver get out of their seat. Because I don't think they could get out of their seats. All of the drivers were what Mom would kindly describe as fleshy. They were big boned men. Who seemed permanently wedged behind the steering wheel, a merger of their flesh with the mechanical navigational infrastructure.

Maybe oversized bodies were a job requirement. Perhaps a fitting was part of the hiring process. Or maybe drivers grew into the job. Normal bodies, re-shaped after years of sitting, and became career stuck. This may sound like I'm throwing bus drivers under the bus. But obviously I'm not. How would I unwedge them and lift them to throw them?

The drivers not only physically stayed down, their moods also stayed down. The only words I ever heard them speak were downers—"Hey, turn it down back there. Keep it down. Sit down. Pipe down. Get down, off the bus, last stop." The latter was helpful because the last stop downtown was my stop.

So, while the wheels on the bus went round and round, I usually slept sound, all the way downtown. I safely took six hundred twenty-four bus trips to and from downtown without an incident. I don't even have a single good bus story. Wouldn't you think I'd have at least one adventure to share? But I don't. And I refuse to make anything up. Everything to this point and beyond is absolute fact. Certainly for the most part. At the very least, a lot of it.

ST. DAVE DRIVE

Moroni

Mr. Moroni was standing outside one day when I delivered his paper, and I noticed he was wearing an eye patch. Strange, I thought, why the eye patch? Had he made a career change and went into piracy? Because to my knowledge, only pirates wore an eye patch. Which I thought was cool. I didn't know any pirates.

And he couldn't just be going through an identity crisis because identity crisis hadn't been invented yet and even if it had, it wouldn't have been something I would know about. So, after a couple of days with his new look, my curiosity drove me to ask about the eye patch.

He told me he had athlete's eye. Mrs. Moroni standing next to him nodded agreement. They both seemed a little proud of this. Now I knew about athletes, and Mr. Moroni was not one. And if Mr. M. had an athlete's eye, why would he cover the eye? Few sports are improved with the use of a single eye.

He picked up on my confusion. He told me he had been itching his athlete's foot. Then rubbed his eye. Thus, creating a very rare case of athlete's eye. Mrs. M nodded in confirmation.

Two things, logically of course, popped into my head. First, as I knew he wasn't an athlete, how did he get an athlete's foot? And could an athletic foot so easily be transferred into an athletic eye? And perhaps, through an assembly process, could one construct an athletic body?

I wondered if his self-diagnosis was inaccurate. I developed a more plausible theory. Maybe he had smelly feet. And when he scratched his eyes, he had inadvertently given himself the stink eye. That kinda disgusted me. Which was hard to do. Disgust was an expertise only girls intuitively seemed to have.

Dempsey

Danny Dempsey was the recognized swearing king. A notable achievement given the neighborhood competition. Danny took his swear game to another level. He was a professional. An artist. Several aspects of his skill separated him from the pack—frequency, word diversity, creative combinations, and delivery flow. But perhaps what made him the potty mouth champ was his consistency—regardless of topic, he never said anything without finding a home for a cuss word every three or four words.

An example might help. I'll try to recreate a Danny swear spew. Ignore if you've heard this before. Cover your ears if you're sensitive—don't shoot the messenger.

"So, I tell the fucking prick to turn left and the fucker goes right. What a dumb fuckin' asshole sons-a-bitch..."

OK, I'm gonna stop. Do you really need to hear a litany of swear words? And would you learn new words and, if so, to what benefit? Another reason I'm stopping is I can't adequately impersonate his swearing routines—so to continue would not do justice to Danny's art form.

Butkus

Mr. Butkus was a TV repairman. He had converted his garage into a repair shop. Outside above the shop door was a lit small neon Motorola TV sign. I thought it was pretty cool. And I thought it was even more cool when I learned his commercial signage within a residential neighborhood was a zoning ordinance violation.

Anyway, Mr. Butkus was my only customer who reciprocated my visits—he was a TV doctor who made house calls. When our TV got sick, we called Dr. Butkus. Then one day, after his thorough exam, he removed his stethoscope and said he can't find a pulse. There's nothing he can do.

Our TV had died. I remember it was a sad day. But what I also remember was when he had bent over during his examination, he presented a "buttcrack" visual. That was notable. Not his partial butt, the fact that I had always understood only plumbers had that exclusive right.

Of course, henceforth, Mr. Butkus became *Mr. Buttcrack* to me. Now one of the risks of kids' secret nicknames for adults was the potential slipup. And despite my careful attention, one evening after Mr. Butkus paid me, I said thanks *Mr. Buttcrack*.

There was no reaction from Mr. Butkus. Maybe because I said this as I was turning to walk away, combined with my likely usual mumbled delivery, he didn't hear my faux pas.

But later I thought about what it would be like to grow up with a *butt* in your name. I bet he must have heard all manner of nicknames that he long ago just stopped paying attention.

Egizio

There were gangs of neighborhood kids, but no neighborhood gangs. There were, however, Greasers. Greasers had greaser hair and wore greaser clothes. In contrast, there were the Surfers. Surfers had surfer hair and wore surfer clothes.

If that doesn't create a mental picture, I'm sorry, but it's the best I got. Partly because I wasn't a Greaser or a Surfer. Who was I? A paperboy, but you already knew that. Anyway, the real difference between the Surfers and the Greasers was dancing. Surfers danced. Greasers didn't dance. (This was pre-Travolta *Grease* & *Saturday Night Fever* movie era.)

Which brings me to Mickey Egizio. Mickey was a hybrid, a Greaser who could dance and did dance. Mickey had all the moves. He could really cut a rug. He did the Twist, Jerk, Monkey, Pony, Swim, Locomotion, Watusi, Nitty Gritty, Mashed Potato, Bird, Limbo, Hitch Hike. He was the Travolta of Sacred Heart neighborhood before there was a John Travolta.

Naturally, all the girls loved Mickey. And obviously, all the guys hated him. But not just because of his dancing. Mickey was also incredibly good looking; movie star stuff.

And speaking of his movie star-ish face, one summer evening, collecting at the Egizio's, Mickey was standing outside. While we exchanged small talk, my shirt suddenly began to flap violently. Mickey instinctively reached into my open shirt and retrieved a moth. I was so relieved my flapping shirt was moth caused and not my rapid heartbeat throb that might suggest I was falling in love with him.

Malinowski

Joey Malinowski introduced me to collecting both stamps and rocks.

One appeal to stamp collecting was how cheap they were—a dime could buy large packets at hobby stores or mail order from the back of comic books. What I found unappealing was that stamps were so abundant. The world supply of stamps seemed infinite, so there was no chance of ever completing the collection, which is a satisfying goal. The other problem with stamp collecting was the challenge to organizing them. There was no simple system.

So shortly after I began to accumulate stamps, I decided to de-accumulate. I quit collecting and gave my unorganized accumulation to a brother. Unlikely, but perhaps had I known FDR was a Philatelic, I might have stuck with it.

Rock collecting held more appeal. Stamps were cheap, but rocks were free. And rocks are more easily organized. Joey's were placed and labeled within empty egg cartons. So, I got an egg carton and I was off to find rocks. I began in the driveway. But I didn't get my rocks off there, only pea gravel.

I hadn't thought something free would be so hard to find. I was unaware of any rock stores, there were no rocks within Cracker Jacks boxes, and Christmas stockings were only filled once a year. I suppose I could've checked back with Joey for rock sources, but I found it easier to just quit. Although not having collected a single rock, technically I never started, so I didn't actually quit, an important technicality because I had started to become concerned with my quitting tendencies.

Romano

Hoarding wasn't prevalent on my paper route, assuming having a bunch of kids doesn't qualify. But the Romano's were suspect. Mr. & Mrs. Romano had a lot of stuff packed floor to ceiling with walking paths, an observation I made when they frequently invited me into their house. But it wasn't just random stuff piles, it was a hoard niche—stacks of newspapers and magazines.

Their stacks were a reference library of previously completed crossword puzzles. The Romano's were serial crossword puzzle solvers, solvers of words that crossed. Although I never once heard them speak cross words, I was pretty sure they had a crossword addiction.

During one of my earliest visits, they asked me if I knew who was known as "The Say Hey Kid." I did, Willie Mays. I think they thought I might be a useful resource. But then I went into a deep slump of word whiffs, swings and misses, and called third strikes before I nailed Henry "Hammering Hank" Aaron. I think the Romano's and I simultaneously reached the same conclusion—my expertise was a narrow niche of famous professional baseball players nicknames.

So, I went from an everyday puzzler player to become a Romano pinch hitter. When needed, I came off the bench to solve Ernie "Mr. Cub" Banks, Ted "The Splendid Splinter" Williams, Joe "The Yankee Clipper" DiMaggio, Stan "The Man" Musial, Larry "Yogi" Berra, and Harmon "The Killer" Killebrew.

Lewendowski

I wasn't much of a fighter. Sure, I've thrown a spitball in my day, but I've never thrown a punch. But I did receive one. Well, sorta, because it was actually a slap from Larry Lewendowski.

Briefly, here's what happened. I flirted with his girlfriend, Mary McFarland. Then Mary told Larry I hit on her. He then hit on me. And told me to stay away from his girl.

Now I'm not sure why Mary told Larry. But I think she did because I may have insulted her with my pathetic flirt. So pathetic she might have felt disrespected. Maybe she thought she deserved my best effort flirt without her knowing that I not only didn't have a top-notch flirt to give her, I didn't even know I had flirted with her.

As I continued to analyze the flirt fight, I thought she should have been even more disrespected by Larry's weak defense of his girl—a mere slap, and not a crisp one either—a backhand that barely brushed my cheek. It was an insult to her girlfriend status. And not just insulting to her, insulting to me too. His slap felt like a dismissal of me as a threat to his girl ownership. I thought I deserved at least a punch.

My final analysis of the incident, on a scale of 1 to 10, my flirt was about a 2. Larry's girlfriend defense maybe a 3. And I think both of those ratings are generous.

Ventino

Mr. Ventino was a regular at Andy's Tavern, where I preferred to collect the Ventino family paper payment. So I could avoid Mrs. Ventino. Which suggests something unsavory about Mrs. Ventino. But not so. In fact, she was just the opposite. Mrs. V smothered me in kindness.

When I collected at the Ventino residence, Mrs. V always invited me into their tiny, immaculate house with her standard greeting—Come in, sweetie, how are you darling, accompanied with a hug. Let me wipe my hands and fix you a plate. You look like you never eat. You sit down here. Her need to feed me was not easily fought off.

Another aspect to the collection routine was Mrs. V's struggle to find her purse—Now where did I put my purse? Mary honey, where's Mama's purse? Mary was her daughter, a couple years younger than me.

Ma, it's where you left it.
I know honey, but where is that?
How do I know?
Be a nice daughter now and help your mama.

And Mary, a nice daughter, would help her mama. And emerge with her purse. And as Mary turned to retreat to her bedroom, she would mumble, leave him alone, Ma. It had no effect on Mrs. V's behavior, but I appreciated Mary's effort.

And then there was Mrs. V's signature goodbye. How's your family, honey? Such nice people, your family. Now you live over on the Sacred Heart Street? You go to the Sacred Heart? And etcetera.

Now based upon the above sketchy information, you might think I was an ungrateful paperboy. And you might be correct. But in my defense, six years with Mrs. V was a long time.

Fitzgerald

As far as I knew, my customer marriages were happy. Or at least civilized. Now maybe some weren't and it's possible I simply didn't notice or, the marital discord was well hidden.

But was there an exception? Always. The Fitzgeralds. It was hard to miss Mr. & Mrs. Fitzgerald's dissonance. They made no effort to hide their battles. They were conducted publicly.

Someone suggested their marriage was doomed from the start—he was Irish, she was Italian and there was something about a water and oil mixture I didn't understand.

Their disharmony were spoken spats that utilized two different verbal weapons. Mrs. F. deployed a rapid-fire word machine-gun. But her aim was either amiss or, maybe Mr. F wore a word-proof vest. Because Mr. F didn't go down.

Mr. F would respond to the assault with a single shot word pistol, firing a "whatever" bullet. The pistol wasn't loud. Maybe it had a silencer. And it may have possibly been defective, because Mrs. Fitzgerald was never silenced and she never went down, but her response volume went up. She reloaded with a verbal litany delivered in Italian. And that was usually successful bringing Mr. Fitzgerald down—down to Andy's Tavern for the evening.

One Saturday morning I had to wade through a clothing heap on their sidewalk to deliver their paper. I didn't examine the apparel closely, but it appeared to belong to Mr. Fitzgerald. On Sunday morning, his haberdashery was gone, a likely temporary ceasefire truce, I assumed.

Kelly

Patrick Kelly was the first kid who seemed to have a career path at an early age. He chose law enforcement, and he contributed to law and order in the neighborhood.

As I walked down a sidewalk one afternoon, delivering papers, Patrick approached me from the opposite direction on his bicycle, dressed in an outfit that resembled a police uniform. Nearly abreast of each other, he spoke into a pretend radio microphone, requesting backup assistance with the sidewalk traffic jam.

Then he stopped me.

What's in the bag?
Newspapers.
Where'd you get them?
Newspaper office.
Ok, move along, nothing to see here.

When I collected at the Kellys, Patrick always answered the door.

No loitering allowed.
I'm collecting for the paper.
ID.
Route 242.
Where were you last Wednesday?
I don't remember.
What did you do to Bob?
He retired.

Now this behavior by Patrick might seem like creative kids' fun. But by age fourteen, clearly not normal. A little odd. Patrick was a challenged kid—something was amiss. But he was completely harmless. And the neighborhood kids knew Patrick had issues, so it was understood it was unfair to mess with Patrick—nobody gave him a hard time.

But that rule was unknown outside the neighborhood. Like at Brother Pasta High School, where both Patrick and I attended. Freshman year, between classes, within the crowded chaotic hallway, headed to my next class, I caught a glimpse of Patrick out of the corner of my eye. He was pinned against his locker by two bullies.

I knew he needed my help, but I was running late, and I didn't stop. Ever wish you had a do over? That was one of mine.

Robertson

Here's to you Mrs. Robertson, paperboy loves you more than you will know, wo, wo, wo.

During the summer, I occasionally collected payment on weekday afternoons. On one sunny warm afternoon, I noticed something different about Mrs. Robertson. Sometime between my thirteenth and fourteenth birthday, she had clearly changed.

She came to her door in a one-piece black swimsuit and invited me into her house. When she turned to retrieve her money was when I noticed how she had changed. Her legs had become far more interesting. And even more so where her swimsuit had slid up the back of her legs, briefly exposing the bottom portion of her body that connects to the top of her rear legs.

Yes, Mrs. Robertson changed from a customer to a work of art. She had become so fine, she had whipped a double eyed whammy on me, to borrow from an old blues song.

And Mrs. Robertson's change also changed me. I altered my summer collection routine to try and sync up the same weekday, time, and weather conditions to return to Mrs. Robertson. Alas, there were no further Mrs. Robertson skin scans—sadly, never a skin sequel show.

Now at that point, I had been a member of a couple of clubs—a smoking club; a drinking club. But I had never started a club. Never been in a leadership role, and I thought it might be time to do so. Because I felt I was ready. My first kiss was under my belt, I had found out how babies were born, and I had started to take matters into my own hands. I had discovered masturbation.

With those credentials and Mrs. Robertson's assistance, unbeknownst to her, I formed a new club. My mental marriage club.

Members had to be between ages thirteen and eighteen, Mrs. Robertson granted an executive exception. And I had to have at one time spoken with the member, but if not, then I had to at the very least be aware of them.

Membership rapidly expanded. And even though the mental marriage club was open to both boys and girls, for some reason, I ended up being the only boy member.

Unlike most clubs, we never met as a group. Meetings were one-on-one sessions only. Because successful marriages need alone time to blossom. But one challenge was finding an appropriate private meeting space. I considered the laundromat and the alley behind the church. Both were unsuitable. I finally decided to make a mental house purchase.

The house provided the privacy that allowed my bride and I to do whatever we wanted to do. Like play all day. And for maximum play comfort, maybe we would like to remove our clothes. And it seems we always wanted to comfortably play all day without clothing. Until death do us part. Which happened at an alarming rate.

Mahoney

Before most of us become self-conscious, early grade school provides everyone an equal opportunity to figuratively step onto the stage, be yourself, do what feels natural, and bask in the limelight of brief notoriety, desired or not. Nothing particularly unique, just the usual five or six-year-old antics—like an unprovoked sudden crying outburst, or maybe a random peeing episode, perhaps a spontaneous vomit.

But one day in first grade, Dick Mahoney went beyond fleeting fame. His performance achieved heroic status, and, with concern about overstating this incident, legendary acclaim.

As the rest of the class was academically toiling, Dick and Diane were partying rather than working. Our nun sent both to the hallway with their crayon cigar box. Hallway rehab was standard punishment. Usually just boys. Anyway, Diane quickly scurried back into the classroom to excitedly report that Dick had run away.

When someone shouted there he goes—the entire class went to the windows to watch Dick running down the street. The girls, in shock at this chaos, looked to our nun to restore crumbling world order. The boys, with noses pressed to the glass pane, cheered—See Dick run. Run Dick run. This was the first real-world application of academic theory.

This was a brazen revolt by Dick against the tyranny of coloring between lines, sequencing letters and numbers, and mandatory floor napping. Apparently, Dick was apprehended because he was back in class the next day. But he was no longer just Dick. He was a newly designated full-blown exalted hero.

Now I should mention Dick had a speech impediment. He stuttered. Nothing crazy, but he struggled a little to get words to exit. Remarkably, following his prison break, a stuttering outbreak began. And strangely, only with boys. And although every boy tried, not all mastered stuttering, to their disappointment.

That stuttering epidemic and Dick's hero status, fondly referred to as the "Dick Era," slipped into the past, with only the occasional nostalgic "remember when Dick." But this was not the end of Dick. Several grades later, Dick made a heroic comeback.

Our seventh-grade nun teacher had stepped out of the classroom. Dick, seated nearest the door, started to play catch with himself by tossing an apple into the air. Each successive toss gained altitude. But on his final fruit loft, not quite hitting the ceiling, it de-lofted too far behind him. And precisely as our nun reentered, the Garden of Eden red orb concluded its descent perfectly atop her habit-covered head.

Now I don't care who you are, that was funny. Unless you were a nun. You could peel the apple tension as we awaited her reaction. Then, incredibly, she started to laugh. This was shocking. There had never been a verified sighting of a laughing nun. Was laughter, like chastity, an abstinence vow? Dick had singularly produced a Catholic miracle and had rightly regained his hero status and a well-deserved end to this memory.

O'Leary

The O'Learys had seven kids and a dog. They were just the nicest people, dog included. If Google existed then, a "nice family" search would have likely produced an O'Leary result.

And that thought triggered this thought—what was my definition of a good paper customer? I knew but decided to formally construct a comprehensive list of criteria from a Tom memory search.

Good paper customers…

- Are never critical about when or where their paper was delivered.
- They didn't hint or suggest they missed Bob.
- My cutting across their tiny yard was allowable.
- Someone was always home to pay me whenever I got around to collecting.
- I was never asked to come back another day for payment.
- Preferably they didn't have a dog, or it was at least restrained for my safety.
- The family were nice, pleasant people.
- One or more of the female family members were pretty.

Most of the above could be ignored if they consistently tipped me. (Side note: when the paper was 40 cents per week, several customers paid me with two quarters or a half-dollar and told me to keep the change. When the paper price went up to 45 cents, my tips were cut in half.)

After writing that, I wondered if my customers had a criterion list for a good paperboy? If so, it was unlikely I would meet many of their expectations.

Back to the O'Learys, they weren't *good* customers. They were *great* customers—they checked off all the boxes. Which leads me to this universal question. Why do bad things seem to happen more frequently to good people?

One cold night, shortly before Christmas, the O'Leary house caught on fire. I stood in the street, near the family and other neighbors, watching firefighters pour water on their home. It was very sad. Made sadder when a young kid innocently said to a parent, loud enough for the O'Leary family to hear, let's go. This isn't fun anymore.

I won't leave you hanging. The fire fighters were on it, minimizing the damage, and a few months later, the O'Learys moved back into their restored home.

Williams

The O'Leary fire was contained and didn't affect the Williams house next door.

Mr. Williams, a bachelor, was possibly my most unique customer in several ways. He was my only customer to address me as *Mr. Thomas*. Only nuns called me Thomas. But never *Mr. Thomas*, and never within a good context. And nuns never pronounced Thomas like Mr. Williams did—miss-ta-toe-moss—stretching and elongating my name by adding extra syllables, enunciated in an up and down harmonious, rhythmic, cadence with a fluid delivery. He created an oral art form out of my simple common name. I liked that.

Because he didn't own a car, he walked to the neighborhood stores, and to the bus stop for non-walkable destinations. He frequently wore a suit and bowtie. In part because of those reasons he was a recognized presence not only on my paper route streets, but he was also likely the most familiar person in the entire neighborhood.

But likely the biggest reason Mr. Williams was so well known was because he was the only black person in our nearly pure Caucasian Sacred Heart neighborhood. He was a bit of a mystery. How did he get into the neighborhood, and even more so, why would he want to?

Although Mr. Williams and I had an easygoing relationship, I didn't feel comfortable asking him about the mystery. But I knew Mr. Williams taught sociology at a local community college—known as junior colleges at the time—and as I think about it now, I wonder if he moved into the Sacred Heart neighborhood to do some sort of sociological research into race.

During my last two summers as a paperboy, Adonis, his niece, began to appear occasionally. She came to help Mr. Williams around the house. Adonis was two years older than me. My experience with Black girls was less than minimal. My guess was her experience with White boys was also likely rare.

We slowly became more comfortable with each other. And one day she introduced the topic of race. She told me she never knew a Black boy named Tommy. And I shared that I had never known a White girl named Adonis.

After this initial ice breaker, Adonis became a little bolder. She asked me why do all white boys look alike? That was funny. We laughed. Because she knew that I knew that she knew, etc., that White people thought all Blacks looked the same. Then she added, now those Chinese people *really* look alike. That was even funnier.

One day I told Adonis she had cool hair. She told me it was an Afro. I said I thought I might try that hairstyle. She told me good luck. Afros were unique to Black people. And then she added, you're not too bright, are you? I said no, if you're talking about my skin sheen. But what if I color my face with black paint like White people did in old movies?

Then Adonis became even bolder—she asked me if all White boys had tiny "tools." Her disguised word didn't confuse me, and I said wow, that was below the belt, but how would I know? And I asked her if all Black girls had big butts? She smiled as she did a little shimmy and said Black boys liked big booties.

We had fun with our candid, sophisticated humor. And it was then that I decided it was time to integrate my mental marriage club—Adonis and I mentally married.

Quigley

The Quigleys had two boys. When their son Jimmy was seven and Franky nine, the Quigleys did an impressive property renovation. They replaced their gravel driveway with concrete—a notable display of wealth—no other customer had a concrete drive.

But that was just the foundation. They then installed not one, but two basketball hoops—one on the garage front and one on the back of their garage. The crowning jewel was a flood light above both.

The engineering was well thought out but maybe one other aspect of their project was not. If the Quigleys intent and vision for their new hoops' mecca was solely for their two young boys' enjoyment, that didn't happen. I don't think Mr. & Mrs. Quigley were familiar with the adage "Build it and they will come." Because we did come, and rarely left. Many kids hung out at all hours to play hoops at the Quigley outdoor basketball arena. The flood light enabled night games into deep darkness.

This ongoing kid presence was likely neither anticipated nor appreciated. When Mrs. Quigley called her boys in for lunch and/or dinner, she probably expected everyone to leave. But subtlety is rarely effective with kids, notably young boys. And Mr. & Mrs. Quigley were too nice to just tell everyone to scram.

So stronger hints began to appear. Their car was parked in the drive more frequently. That had some impact, but there was always the rear backup hoop. Then the spot light was lit less often. And then subtlety disappeared entirely—the backup rear hoop was removed followed shortly thereafter by the disappearance of the front basket.

Without the hoops, we got the message—take your game elsewhere. The concrete drive was all that remained from their project, but for what purpose I wouldn't know.

White

One late afternoon delivering papers, I heard an unusual noise. The source of this unidentifiable racket came from the White's garage. Where I found Joey White and two other guys with musical instruments—a trombone, accordion, and a cowbell—attempting to play music. I would not have guessed.

Joey asked if I recognized the song. Oh yes, the title is on the tip of my tongue. Joey told me it was "Jailhouse Rock," an instrumental version. I had zero recognition of the Elvis classic. But worse, they asked what I thought. I asked about what. What did I think of their music? Oh, incredible, I lied with my reply.

Technically, it wasn't a lie. It was incredible. Incredibly bad. But I was no music critic. Maybe their jazz interpretation didn't work for an Elvis tune.

My enthusiastic response may have been too enthusiastic. And perhaps my uncoordinated finger snapping to their song implied I was a musician, because Joey invited me to join their band. Although I was flattered, I wasn't sure I wanted in. So, I told Joey I didn't have an instrument, the assumption that was the only obstacle to joining and making a contribution. Joey said just get one. Well, I said, what instrument would best blend into your signature sound? He said we could always use more cowbell, but really, any instrument would work.

So, I said I probably would. Joey then said stick around, we're gonna play "Silent Night." I'd love to, I said, but maybe another time, I have papers to deliver.

A few days later Joey told me the band had disbanded because of artistic differences. He seemed despondent. Too bad, and I'm surprised, I said, you guys sounded tight.

McPherson

Mr. McPherson was a friendly guy. He was a boy scout leader, and he enthusiastically encouraged me to join his scout troop. I told him I had never completed cub scouts. He told me that it could be worked around. Then I told him my school, paper route, and sports prevented additional activities.

But I had other reasons why I didn't want to be a boy scout. My struggles with gluing in cub scouts provided me no desire for advanced gluing in boy scouts. And I had heard boy scouts did Jamboree's. Even though I didn't know what a Jamboree was or what happened at Jamboree's, I just didn't see myself as a Jamborean.

And sleeping on the ground in a tent held little appeal. Actually, none.

It was kind of Mr. McPherson to encourage my scouthood. At the time, I felt a little bad for my rejection of his invitation. But now I consider it good luck. Because many years later, Mr. McPherson was rumored to have had some creative fun with some of his scouting boys on those overnight Jamboree's.

Now I realize this is a little weird, but I have to admit that Mr. McPherson's interest in me took a little sting out of my priest snubs. It always feels good to be desired.

Santorini

I never cut through the yard to the Santorini house. The reason I never cut through the yard was because I couldn't. The property was entirely engulfed in a small jungle. So, I had to walk around on the sidewalk, and I couldn't even toss the paper toward the front stoop because I couldn't accurately throw it through the narrow opening of the overgrowth.

And so my paper delivery to Mr. Santorini, the elderly bachelor house inhabitant, was not efficient. But Mr. Santorini made up for this inefficiency when I collected from him. He was a man of few words, and so our verbal interactions were always brief.

Brief was nice, but it was his *always* I most appreciated. His consistency. I could always rely on Mr. Santorini's predictable behavior. I've never been a fan of surprises. Nothing about Mr. Santorini ever surprised me.

For example, he wore the same clothes every day. Perhaps he had no other clothing. But uniforms were not uncommon, attire often dictated by schools and workplaces. So it could have been that his clothing was his home uniform.

Even more common than uniforms was smoking. Mostly cigarettes. A couple customers smoked cigars. A few pipe men. Snuff and chew were rare. Mr. Santorini was always smoking a cigarette. In six years, I never once saw him without a smoke in either his hand or hanging from his lips. He was an urban version of the Marlboro Man. But he didn't smoke Marlboro's. His brand was Lucky Strikes, a non-filtered real man's smoke.

Because of our weekly exchange of money, I had the opportunity, but rarely noted, details of my customer's fingers and hands. But Mr. Santorini's fingers were notable for their orange/yellow discoloration from his smoking, as was his mustache, similarly stained.

The other noticeable result of his smoking was his consistent smell. His *uniform*, body, breath, and house had a smoke reek, which I found endearing for the consistency—I never had to guess what he might have eaten or cooked for dinner—no other aroma ever had a chance against the smoke stink.

For some reason, that smoke stench strength was not strong enough to prevent my decision to start smoking.

Lucas

Following our Sacred Heart eighth grade graduation ceremony, some of us guys were hanging out in the parking lot. Reflecting upon our achievement, and for some, grammar school completion was an unexpected success.

Mike Lucas broke our silent glory bask. He said let's play golf tomorrow. Silence returned. Golf? Someone said tell us more. Surprisingly, Mike's golf idea was embraced. I suppose with grade school diploma's secured, we were like *what else ya got life? —bring it on.*

The next day we announced at the club house we were there to play golf. The attendant thanked us for the clarification. With our rented clubs and other weaponry, we went to the first tee as a nine-some and launched our inaugural golf shots, although launching might be a stretch—few balls got airborne. Whiffing a stationary ball is inherently hilarious and although we were bad golfers, we were decent trash talkers—*stick to jacks, jack off*—that sort of banter.

We hacked our way and holed out hole one. Everyone scored double digits, twenty-three the worst, and likely the most accurate and honest. Billy, through a combination of bad math, bad memory, and good cheating, announced a group best ten. That generated a collective, spontaneous *bullshit*—he immediately caved and said give me a fourteen—and even that was highly suspect.

Now I wasn't class valedictorian, so I can't speak for the golf group. But I suspect most viewed the day as a one and done activity. Myself? I was hooked—not sure about lined and sinkered—but very pleased, and a little impressed with my 178 strokes score. By summer's end, I had busted through the 150-stroke barrier, and with paper route wealth, bought my own clubs.

Andrysiak

As I stated at the beginning, every customer had something unique about them. Most of that uniqueness was usually a family member. But in the case of the Andrysiak family, it was their house.

Their house style was like most other houses, but the exterior color was uniquely eye grabbing. Or more accurately, eye blinding. It was a remarkably bright, glowing, yellow hue. If you've ever stared at a plate of lightly scrambled eggs after dropping some acid or other form of a hallucinogen, you can picture what I'm describing.

If not, then maybe try thinking of some extroverted banana whose yellow skin just kind of got away from them—their yellow screaming—*you think you know yellow? You want yellow? You can't handle yellow.*

Still no mental picture? Sorry. You're on your own. That's all I got.

Now because of neighborhood segregation, the token minority houses were frequently used as geographic reference points. For example, across the street from the Black guy, a block over from the Chinaman, two doors down from the Jews.

But the Andrysiak house was the most cited geographic landmark—take a right at the yellow house.

Petrosky

The Petroskys had no children. Mr. Petrosky worked at a factory. Mrs. Petrosky took care of some neighborhood kids—she was available without notice for drop offs.

Mrs. Petrosky, or "Bobbi" as she preferred, was my favorite female adult customer. Bobbi did household things usually performed by men. She not only mowed the lawn, she maintained the mower. And she changed the oil and tuned up their car.

She had a great tool belt and within their garage, a work bench with tools neatly hung from a peg board. And Bobbi showed me how some of her tools worked. Memorable tutorials—not because I retained anything—memorable for her kind attention.

At some point I learned Mr. Petrosky wasn't Bobbi's husband. He was her brother. And still later, I heard some older kids refer to her as the "dyke." At age eleven, I didn't know what that meant, but I do remember it didn't sound flattering. Then when I found out the meaning, I was a little confused. I wondered why liking women was considered a bad thing. Why wouldn't everyone like women? I still wonder.

Kelsey

Katie Kelsey was a member of my mental marriage club. But in real life, we were mere acquaintances, an odd but accurate description of our teenage relationship.

Anyway, one day, when we were about fourteen, Katie told me something truly startling. She said some girl liked me. That was stunning news that totally blew me away.

But that was just my inner reaction. My external response to Katie was a little different. I responded with complete indifference. I thought I did a convincing impersonation of a yawning, bored, couldn't care less guy. Her information was not surprising, I said. Girls are always falling for me. Tell her to take a number and get in line—I'm totally not interested.

As I turned to walk away, I said, just for the hell of it, who is she? Katie said she couldn't tell me—she had sworn to secrecy. My nonchalant, cool façade melted into a lukewarm pathetic puddle. I collapsed. Crumbled. Unraveled. My façade replaced by a full blown grovel. I begged Katie to reveal the Like-me-girl. It was an embarrassing, shameless, display. But Katie wouldn't budge. Maybe because we were mere acquaintances.

It was a strange feeling being a person of notice. And it created some serious self-awareness anxiety, an uncomfortable discomfort. Because I loved my anonymity. Probably because I was good at it. Rarely paid attention to, I was comfortable with my no notice existence by everyone and everywhere—school, sports, family.

My only experience with notoriety was my Little League home run.

My homer wasn't a classic dig in at the plate, time a fastball perfectly, and rip a rocket into the horizon. Somehow my bat met the ball, sending a lazy fly ball riding on a gale force wind over the fence. I was shocked. It was so completely unexpected, I didn't know whether to walk, run, trot, stroll, or any other descriptors for post-home run movement. I don't remember Coach Lollar teaching us the appropriate home run response. Or if he did, I likely didn't see the relevance to me.

In the days that followed my home run, I understood what it might feel like to be a celebrity. Now nobody actually said anything, but I picked up on my customers' nuanced glances. They clearly no longer saw me as just Tommy the paperboy—they saw Tommy the home run king. That made me uncomfortable, but I rode out the storm and it soon faded away.

I tried to figure out why a girl would like me. What about me did my undeclared girlfriend like? Girls consistently confused me. All I knew was girls liked guys without a belly button (Mickey Murphy), with bad acne (Tom Quinn), and could dance (Mickey Egizio). What did I have? Slim Jim breath?

Even though she was a mystery, she was real. *Documented.* This was a game changer. My first move? I disbanded my mental marriage club. That was child's play. Fantasy. A real girl was now my romantic partner. And my second move was to figure out how not to blow it.

Katie wouldn't reveal the identity of my hidden girlfriend. But I respected my anonymous admirer's desire for anonymity. We can work around that. And then I had a lightbulb moment. Is it possible that Katie was my secret admirer? I mean, girls are crafty.

So, I asked Katie. And she immediately launched into a lengthy belly laugh, finally catching her breath long enough to say maybe in your dreams. Wow. She knew about my mental marriage club? Girls were so smart.

My mystery romance was short. One day Katie told me to forget about Like-me-girl. My unidentified girlfriend had found a new boyfriend. I guess I did blow it. Without any effort. But I remembered the expression when life hands you a lemon, make some orange juice. I re-convened my mental marriage club—minus Katie—we divorced, and reverted to acquaintances.

PAPER OFFICE

It was a three-block walk from my downtown bus stop to the paper office. Initially, I was vigilant on this trek as I carried my significant money stash. But soon it became apparent there was no danger—Saturday morning downtown wasn't entirely a ghost town, but it was definitely lightly populated.

The newspaper headquarters was within a six-story, brick monstrosity that took up a full city block, the largesse necessary because it housed the printing presses. The building was a serious structure that would have likely survived an earthquake, or even a Russian sneak attack.

Carrier entry was through a darkened, gritty alley at the rear of the building. The short walk included passing by an old wino. He was either passed out on, or covered by, some filthy blankets or, sometimes, he sat slumped against the building wall.

Everyone called him Gooseneck. Early on, I observed some older paperboys' interactions with him. If he was conscious, Gooseneck would verbally taunt the carriers with a barely coherent *get out of my house*. And some of the carriers would reply with some variation of *shut the fuck up Gooseneck or I'll smash your wine bottle, after I empty it.*

Regardless, if Gooseneck was awake or passed out, and regardless if there was any verbal exchange, there was a tradition that everyone threw some coins near him before entering the building. I never verbally engaged Gooseneck, but I always donated.

All carriers entered through a door with an old rusted "carrier only" sign hung above it. My early walks down that alley and through that door were exciting. I felt like a celebrity actor or a famous musician who never arrived through front doors like the patrons, but always had special access through a restrictive entry. I had that sense I was a member of an exclusive, private club.

But that special feeling soon waned, well before my six-year, weekly stint ended. The glamor eroded entering the narrow low lit drab hallway that led to the equally non-descript payment space. Standing in line with my peers, there was nothing to suggest I was rubbing elbows with celebrities.

And the crabby cashier woman never greeted me as someone special.

Next. Route number?

242.

I then slowly dumped my large collection of coins into the spinning coin counting machine. After the metal money was tabulated, I paid the balance with the paper money, mostly one-dollar bills, an occasional five, and less frequently, two-dollar bills that were still in circulation.

SACRED HEART STREET

Folsom

Bob Folsom, several years older, introduced me to coin collecting. The paper route generated a lot of coins, so it was a nice hobby fit.

Early in my numismatic pursuit, I struck up a business relationship with Joe the Ice Cream Man. Joe had the ice cream route in the Sacred Heart neighborhood. Like my business, Joe's business handled a lot of coins. Mid-week, we made a money exchange—I gave him $20; he gave me a huge bag of pennies. I would then search the bag for rare finds, and on Friday night, I would return the pennies, squaring up any difference.

Now Joe didn't peddle his ice cream on a pedaled bicycle with a manual bell ringer. He drove a brightly lit, music-blaring truck. There was nothing subtle about his presence—a commercial jet landing would have been more discreet. Although it was impossible to miss Joe's appearance, one Friday night I managed to do just that.

And so Saturday morning, I had to lug that heavy penny bag onto the bus, and then to the paper office where I began to empty the Lincoln cents into the coin counting machine. I had to slowly penny pour because the quantity of my small denomination of official U.S. minted metal overwhelmed the machine. The sluggish initial response to its penny counting job became even more sluggish, and I think not just because of the sheer volume. I think it reacted to its task with a bad attitude that turned into an intentional work slowdown.

Its slowdown response had a ripple effect that caused my carrier peers queue to back up, out the door, into the alley. There was an escalation of audible discontent. It wasn't pretty. And that non-pretty turned ugly when combined with the always crabby clerk verbally cranking her crabby to a heightened level of vocal crabbiness.

Joe and I abandoned our short-lived money exchanges. The paper office fiasco certainly contributed to the demise, but more so my decision to abandon the coin collecting hobby. That move was driven mostly because my poor cash flow management generated more coin removals from my collection than coin additions.

Restoni

Mr. Anthony Restoni was a politician. But he wasn't elected. He was appointed by his neighbors, dubbed the Mayor of Sacred Heart Street.

The mayor became mayor because of his strong opinions, viewpoints he delivered in front of his house to anyone who happened by. Like his paperboy, who happened by every day. And as a member of the press, my appearance sufficed for the mayor's impromptu press conferences. There were no press questions because these were not media Q & A's—these were rant-like sermons preached by Mayor Restoni.

The mayor's ranting topics were all manners of ills, corruption, and ineptitudes of elected officials—terrible snow removal, shitty garbage collection, bad street cleaning, un-repaired potholes, and runaway park district taxes were some of his frequent favorites. He also liked to go on about the general demise of society. Notably, the neighborhood going down the shitter with riff raff moving in, but the Irish never moving out.

Kids were a recurring rant—lazy, jaywalking, sidewalk spitting hooligans, spoiled by parents sparing the rod. And gutless teachers who never flunked students deserving to be held back, passing kids through grades like a Drano-greased drainpipe. The mayor loved to tell his Billy story as proof of the benefit of flunking. Apparently his classmate Billy Bono flunked fourth grade and went on to become a surgeon. He lamented the loss of inspirational flunked but succeeded kids.

Mayor Restoni frequently wondered how Buttcrack (Mr. Butkus, the TV repair man) got away with a commercial neon sign in the neighborhood? And what the hell happened to Latin that was once spoken at Mass? Where did milk delivery go? Mail delivery stinks. Paper delivery the worst.

Paper delivery? Hold on there, your honor, I didn't say but thought. Because I never challenged the mayor, except when he said how much he missed Bob, my predecessor. Well, I refused to let him get away with that. It was a personal attack, and I would not stand for that—no sir, I walked away. But I don't think he noticed my departure because I could still hear him verbally ramble on as I physically rambled on.

Longley

In the summer when I was eleven, Don Longley taught me and other kids how to play poker. Don was two years older, an only child of working parents. His parental absence provided the venue and opportunity to run his penny ante poker games.

He had strict house rules—only pure poker—five-card draw, five and seven-card stud. No wild card stuff. Swearing was allowed, but no trash talk, whining, or crying. If someone's luck was down, Don gave them more pennies. Because for Don, it was more of a social activity than a gambling event.

And it was Don's ability as a host that made it special. He served drinks, snacks, and played some great music, spinning his stack of 45 RPM records on his portable record player—Dion, Shirelles, Supremes, Temptations, Ray Charles, Neal Sedaka, and Chubby Checker all come to mind—but absolutely no Country.

Nordstrom

The Nordstrom family had five kids, four boys and a girl—Mary, a couple years older than I, and very cute—which of course meant she always ignored me. That seemed to happen frequently with girls and more frequently with cute girls for some reason.

I would see three of her four brothers off and on, but I knew there was another boy that I had never seen. Until one summer day, Mrs. Nordstrom was outside when I delivered the newspaper. She was standing next to this son, who was slumped in a wheelchair, his body severely deformed, his head hanging down nearly to his chest.

Mrs. Nordstrom was pouring some fluid down a flexible tube that disappeared beneath his shirt. Foolishly, I asked Mrs. Nordstrom what was wrong with him. And Mrs. Nordstrom, usually pleasant to me, replied tersely and briefly, nothing.

Mahler

One day after finishing my paper delivery, I ran into Jerry Mahler carrying fishing gear. And he invited me to join him. My fishing experience at age twelve was limited. Actually, never.

Jerry was a grade ahead of me. Until that point in time, I had a singular knowledge of Jerry. During the 1960 presidential election between Nixon and Kennedy, my class sat in on Jerrys' class mock presidential debate. Jerry portrayed Nixon. Late in the debate, the JFK guy shared compelling data on the alarming number of kids in America who went to bed hungry.

Nixon was Ike's VP and as the incumbent, this was on his watch. So, I thought Jerry's candidate was doomed. But Jerry retorted that most of those kids were sent to bed hungry as punishment for bad behavior. To me, that was sheer brilliance. And based upon that, I projected Jerry's fishing brilliance and accepted his fishing offer.

We walked a long way to an abandoned factory. Jerry told me it had once made horse buggy whips. I wondered why it had closed. Anyway, at the rear of the building was an opening through a rusted metal fence to a path that led us to the shores of a small body of water. I knew it wasn't a lake, but it might have qualified for pond status.

Jerry baited the hook on his rod and reel from a small paper bag. It was bread scrunched into a tiny sphere held together by some moisture agent. He told me it was a dough ball. As he cast, I sat, swatting mosquitoes. We may have tripped a mosquito "fresh meat" alarm.

He re-cast and I re-swatted. And he re-cast. And re-cast. His casting never produced a fish. Now I don't know if his fishless hook reeling refrain was a result of some flaw in his skill or, perhaps the empty floating beer and pop bottles and partially submerged car tire suggested the fish may have abandoned this home. But it did stimulate this question—

why am I here? This was not an existential query and it did produce an answer. Don't ever go fishing again.

Rosenstein

I think the Rosensteins, Mr. & Mrs., son David and daughter Sara, were a Jewish family. If so, they were my only Jewish customer. I say if so because although others referred to them as Jews, I wasn't sure.

I thought Jews wore black clothes, skull caps, and braided their hair. The Rosensteins didn't do any of that. I had heard Jew in reference to getting a lower price. Or being cheap. But the Rosensteins consistently tipped me. And I thought Jewish was a religion. But how is a religion identified? Does a guy walk into a bar and everyone thinks now there's a Methodist if I ever saw one.

Perhaps I should have just asked them, but I wasn't comfortable doing so. I didn't know how to start that discussion. So, I didn't. And regret not doing so. Because Jewishness still confuses me and remains a bit of a mystery.

Halloran

Did you know September 13 is Blame Someone Else Day? So I blame Johnny Halloran for his influence on my spiritual erosion. It happened as altar boys in sixth grade.

There were a lot of rituals in the Catholic world—perhaps other religions also had many, but I was unaware, maybe because we were told none of them were true religions and thus, we shouldn't know of their pagan details.

Anyway, I think where I'm going with this Johnny Halloran incident occurred during Lent. After Jesus was crucified, his direct flight ascension to heaven was delayed. He hung out in a cave, bodyguards posted to prevent kidnapping. Since then, altar boys have symbolically continued this security detail, I think during Lent.

Altar boys were assigned guard duty in pairs for one-hour stints. I was paired with Johnny one night on the late shift, the 8-9 PM slot. Because that was a slow time for parishioners checking in on the dead Jesus, we were alone in the church, silently and reverently kneeling. Until Johnny became irreverent.

He stood and broke into a little soft shoe dance. Maybe my amused response encouraged him because Johnny then escalated his choreography. He slid across the floor, his arms raised, rendering an impressive James Brown and pre-Michael Jackson moonwalk medley impression, throwing out some Southern Baptist hallelujahs and amen brothers.

We both thought it was thoroughly hilarious. Not because of what he did, but where he did it—in God's house, Jesus up on the altar, within the bastion of Catholicism.

And then the squeaky church front door announced someone had arrived, assumingly to pray and pay respects to the dead Jesus. So, we had to re-grab our reverence. But we had both developed a terrible case of the giggles—the "giddy-up" giggles that couldn't be reined in—like unsuccessfully trying to withhold a sneeze, and when it burst out, it became the loudest most violent sneeze ever.

Johnny went into the sacristy to re-reverate. I had just started to re-compose when he returned, walking in an overly solemn, rigid, devout, folded hands processional paced manner that made me lose it again. I nearly ran to the sacristy to bury my head in the hanging cassocks to muffle my laughter.

Now I'm not certain, but I think Johnny must have confessed this incident to a priest during confession. Because years later, he had entered the seminary, which must have been his penance, and if so, a rather harsh penance in my opinion.

McFarland

The McFarland house was unique because it was the only house with a doorbell. Or the only one I remember. Or maybe the only one that worked. Anyway, it was a real knuckle saver. But the doorbell detail is just a prelude. The real McFarland story is Mary.

I have previously introduced Mary—after I unknowingly flirted with her, her boyfriend, Larry Lewendowski, slapped me. Larry and Mary subsequently broke up and despite our rough start, I thought Mary and I might try a new beginning.

Did I mention earlier that Mary was a real cutie? Which of course qualified her for mental marriage club membership, a seemingly perfect mental spouse fit. But here's what's strange. I just couldn't mentally get Mary and I going. Our bliss was amiss. I mean I tried, but it just wasn't happening.

I considered talking this through with Mary and gave serious thought to mental marriage counseling. But I finally decided to just abandon my effort at trying to make "us" work. I mean, there's only so much a guy can do to keep a mental marriage alive and healthy. Some marriages just flat out don't work.

I felt sorry for Mary—a failed mental marriage so early in her marital career. Hopefully she found happiness within a different mental marriage club.

Simoni

At some point in my six-plus-year paperboy career, I was invited into every customer house. These entries were mostly brief collecting visits with minimal memory of the interior. But the Simoni family's wall hangings left a memorable impression. Their living room walls were covered with paintings. It was a mini art gallery with a Christian religious theme.

The centerpiece was a sizable painting of a well-attended dinner party. Based upon the twelve guests' taut faces, not sure when their last supper was. And there was a portrait of Mary holding a baby in her arms. I frequently studied her face and although I wasn't an art critic, I was pretty sure the artist was not trying to replicate Mona Lisa's generic expression. Mary seemed to me to be struggling to understand how that baby got into her arms and what her next move was.

Within the religious theme was a blood sub-theme—a headshot of Jesus dripping blood from his crown of thorns, a couple of crucifixion renderings with all sorts of blood leaking, flowing, gushing, oozing—the full package, a real tribute to bloodletting.

Mostly the Simoni pictures made me reflect on my good luck—lucky that I didn't live at a time when crucifixions were fashionable and lions ate well; a time when you might just be headed out for an evening stroll and the next thing you know you're randomly chosen for a beheading. I thought then and still do about poor Joan from Arc. She burns one steak and she becomes a burnt steak.

I also wondered if the Simoni collection was merely religious art, or was the painter commissioned to produce religious marketing? Intended to recruit new Christians with a sort of inspirational gore genre. Probably not, and this might be conspiracy theory, but it seems to me Christianity has a violent penchant.

Brzezinski

The Brzezinski family had several kids. All seemed unremarkable to me except for George. A year younger than myself, he just struck me as a little odd. Maybe he was a writer. But let's set that aside for the moment. Or better, permanently. Anyway, one afternoon, after dropping their paper on their porch step, and as I headed toward the next house, George suddenly appeared next to me. I didn't see him approach and he really startled me. After my heart spike went down, my annoyance went up.

And then George threw my natural emotional progression into disarray. He asked if he could blow me. My annoyance shifted to confusion, then stunned, then back to annoyance, then anger. I really didn't appreciate him causing my emotional roller coaster. And I told him in an unkindly manner to get away from me.

Pellegrini

Mr. & Mrs. Pellegrini were retired empty nesters. Mrs. Pellegrini a former nurse, Mr. Pellegrini previously a teacher. Mrs. P. usually answered my door knock. And only she paid me.

When Mr. P. made a rare appearance, he was confused who I was or why I was there. Sometimes he thought I was a student in his class. And sometimes he thought I was there to drop off my essay assignment. Obviously the first time this occurred, I was as confused as he was.

Mrs. Pellegrini would frequently get to the door before it became awkward. And she explained to me that Mr. Pellegrini was a very smart person but had lost much of his memory. I said that's sad. And she said yes, it is.

Melton

Mr. & Mrs. Melton had no children. Mr. Melton worked at a bank. Mrs. Melton was usually at home, and I think she may have been what was referred to as a homemaker.

Mrs. Melton was my most formally groomed customer. She always wore a dress and earrings, fingernails freshly polished, lipstick precisely lipsticked, her hair dramatically doo'd.

Now as I reflect upon the innumerable customer conversations in my paperboy career, one stands out, and no other is even close. It was with Mrs. Melton. She was a pleasant lady whom I had no reason to suspect wasn't a happy person. Until one summer day when she invited me into her pristine home, as she always did, I asked Mrs. M if she liked not having to work.

What was I thinking? As usual, I wasn't. And my seemingly harmless inquiry opened a side of Mrs. Melton previously unseen—Mrs. Melton went into a meltdown. She started calmly by asking me if I knew who did all the house cleaning? I took a stab and said you? Continuing, she asked if I had ever mopped a floor, cleaned a toilet or a bathtub?

She didn't wait for my answer before continuing with her vocal volume raised a couple notches—I do all of that and I dust every square inch of this house, do all the grocery shopping, meal preparation, dish washing, laundry, and ironing.

And while I do all this shit, hubby gets to go banking, doing cool stuff with interesting people, (the timing didn't seem right for me to remind her that she visited with me), then he comes home, plops his ass down on the couch to smoke his pipe, read the newspaper, and sip the Manhattan I made for him while I'm making food for him to not only eat, but also critique.

Just when I thought the end had arrived, Mrs. Melton shifted gears—how would you like to wear this outfit doing all that mundane, disgusting stuff? Everyday. Try wearing high heels delivering the newspaper as she angrily kicked her elevated heels off. Her verbal dress down continued as her dress fell, magically unzipped from the back to reveal a hidden intricate female clothing infrastructure system. Do you think slips, girdles, nylons, bras are fun? Comfortable? Try it sometime.

Thankfully she stopped removing clothing. Because Mrs. Melton, respectfully, was no Mrs. Robertson. When she was apparently done, I thought I should say something. So, I said thank you. She said you're welcome. Now zip me up.

Marino

I had reasonable success at avoiding fights, both verbal and physical. But I managed to get caught up in a tussle with Frank Marino.

One summer day following a pickup baseball game, Frank told me he could run one hundred laps around the baseball field, non-stop. I bet him a quarter he couldn't. What a stupid bet. He barely broke a sweat, easily completing his century circular run. In a feeble attempt to save my wager, I lamely said he had cheated, so the bet was off.

I expected his disagreement. But I didn't anticipate the fervor of his different point of view. His resolution was fisticuffs. He told me he was going to kick my ass. In my best male bravado, borrowed from Mr. Chan, I told him to bring a lunch, it'll be an all-day job. That didn't work, he didn't even flinch. But I did, and I handed him a quarter.

That was the equivalent of not answering the bell and dropped my career fight record to 0-2-1. And that was my final fight. At age thirteen, having never swung a punch, I retired from the fight game, quit the ring, and became a pacifist.

Of course my pacificism didn't extend to family.

Frederickson

This house was a rental property, and people periodically moved in and out. Mr. Frederickson was one of those renters.

Mr. Frederickson, a middle-aged bachelor or divorcee, was rarely at home. So, I had a hard time collecting from him. This missed collection stretched out to seven weeks. Until one early Friday evening I found him there. He apologized for his lack of payment. But if I would be kind enough to wait until tomorrow morning, he would settle with me.

Delivering his Saturday morning paper the next day, he didn't answer my door knock. Then I noticed the curtains no longer covered the windows. And I stared into the vacant house. Really? Who stiffs a paperboy? Frederickson did.

But hang on. Several years later, well after my paperboy days, I ran into Frederickson. I don't remember where. He didn't recognize me, but I refreshed his memory about the debt he owed me. He gave me some pathetic, weak, oversight apology. And then he said wait here, and he'd grab his wallet from his car. I said I'm heading that way, I'll tag along. Oh, no bother, he said, I'll be right back.

I think there's an expression about fool me once and twice, and something about blame and shame. Anyway, I went with him, and he paid me. This restored my faith in fairness. And maybe more so it restored my faith in luck. Regardless, it restored money in my pocket.

Dockendorf

George Dockendorf and I were in Father Martin's freshman English class. It was a good fit—George and I were both lazy students—and Father Martin was a lazy teacher.

But that didn't mean we didn't learn anything. The first thing we learned was that Father Martin was a big sports fan. And then we learned that if you got him talking about sports at the start of class, he never got around to talking about English.

The only real challenge was deciding who would initiate the sports conversation. Because that person had to spend the entire period engaged with Father Martin while everyone else could sleep. So George, myself, and a couple of other guys would decide before class who the designated talk guy would be.

For the most part, we came to agreement, based pretty much on a rotational basis. But inevitably, one day nobody stepped up to the sports topic initiator task. And Father Martin taught English that day. We still slept, but it wasn't as comfortable trying to be discreet. Lesson learned. That never happened again.

Because of the absence of any formal education, there was an equal absence of any grading. One day somebody asked Father Martin about grades. He said that would be fairly addressed at the conclusion to the semester.

And true to his word, on the last day of the semester, he explained how that little messy business of grades would be handled. Father Martin announced that everyone would get a C for a final grade. However, if anyone had an issue with that, come see him after class.

I was impressed with Father Martin's academic integrity. And I briefly considered seeing him after class, but decided the line was too long.

O'Shaughnessy

Mr. & Mrs. O'Shaughnessy were an elderly couple. Their large brood of children had left the nest, I assume as a natural part of maturity.

But I also wondered if their dad may have hastened their departure decision.

Mr. O'Shaughnessy was a walking jokebox. His extensive humor inventory was likely shared over the years with his kids, as he kindly did so with me—every time I saw him—for over six years.

He told long, endless groaners. Like the Tipperary saga, and the shaggy dog epoch. He had multiple versions of guys walking into bars, knock-knock jokes, and old people humor was an oldie but a goodie topic. Gender, sex, handicap, and religion were all well represented.

His racial jokes were prevalent, and ethnic humor was one of his favorites—he spared none—Irish, Italian, Polish—like the two Polish pilots approaching the landing strip repeating their shock at how short the runway was and equally surprised at the width.

Today, Mr. O'Shaughnessy's humor would be primarily viewed as dad jokes. And most of his repertoire would be considered insensitive, politically incorrect, racist, sexist, and all the other *ists*. But that sensitivity had not surfaced back then or, at least not with the larger population, myself included. This doesn't suggest that none of his humor bothered me. It did. But what bothered me was his jokes just weren't that funny.

The lack of humor was probably a combination of bad material combined with my inability to understand most of the jokes. I just didn't get most of them. But I did get that it was rude not to laugh. The challenge was timing my laugh.

Thankfully, Mr. O'Shaughnessy helped me guess when the joke was done. His already reddish face grew redder as the joke progressed, evolving into gut shaking, body convulsing laughter, concluding with his signature signoff, *Schmock, Schmock*—Swedish, he told me, meaning the end.

I remember feeling a little sorry for Mr. O'Shaughnessy. A tinge of sadness that I couldn't really explain or understand. But I clearly understood why I felt sorry for Mrs. O'Shaughnessy.

Grassley

I previously spoke about my collecting time seeping into every night of the week in part because of distractions. Mark Grassley was one of my distractions. When I collected at the Grassley house, it would be my final stop for the night. Because Mark and I would play two unique sports games, our choice was dictated by the season.

In the summer we played wiffle ball. At that point, I considered the wiffle ball to be the best invention of all-time, all inventions considered, not just sports related. I still rank it in the top ten.

The wiffle was a baseball made of plastic with slitted holes that allowed the wind to impede its travel distance, which was perfect for a small-space, two-person baseball game. The wind would also create unpredictable ball movement. Pitching a wiffle ball made you feel like you were Juan Marichal. Unfamiliar with Mr. Marichal? Google him. Well worth the effort.

During winter, we played Nerf hoops. Nerf hoops, or Nerf basketball, was another small space, two-person game. The small Nerf ball was a spongy, flimsy substance perfectly designed to go through the equally small, flimsy, netted hoop hung over the top of Mark's bedroom door.

You didn't shoot the ball into the hoop; you violently slammed it in. Which required pillows, blankets, rugs, coats and anything else available to line and protect the bedroom walls and the door from damage. And protect your body. There were no rules about body contact. Nerf hoops was really more of a football game than basketball. Mark's body was like a human bowling ball. And his power dunks were so nasty, my game goal wasn't winning, it was physical survival.

I always wondered if Bob, my predecessor, was also challenged by distractions.

Callahan

You might remember that I was supposed to count the papers before I began delivery. So if I was short, there was time for the paper office to bring more. I always tried to be generally consistent, and so I consistently never counted the papers.

It was a time saving gamble that usually paid off. But not always. On those rare occasions when I was short, the only solution I had was to skip a house. So, I consistently handled that dilemma by simply rotating the skipped customer. And because it was late in my delivery before I figured out I had more houses remaining than newspapers remaining, the skipped customer was always near the end of my route.

Mr. Callahan lived near that end. And I found out he was a bad skipped choice. After he told me he had not gotten the previous day's paper, he then launched into a lengthy lecture about responsibility. Because I feigned listening to him, it took me a little while to realize he was talking about my responsibility. And that responsibility, he continued, also included getting his Sunday morning paper delivered before noon.

My initial thought was wow, you can't go a single day without the comics? Get a life. But his passion for his beloved periodical elevated my concern. Not a concern for me—for Mr. Callahan. Was he struggling with some larger life issues?

Taking out his frustrations by whining about his missing paper? Was this the proverbial dog kick? But he didn't have a dog. And that explained why my hung head puppy dog response to his lecture was ineffective.

He concluded by saying get your shit together kid. Or so I thought it was his conclusion. He made a final point that none of this happened when Bob had the paper route. Larger life problems or not, that last tag on was so totally unnecessary. Mom would have called it rude. Plus, I had already decided to remove him from the skip rotation.

Detello

Anthony Detello was a year younger than me. A nice quiet kid who was a bit of a loner.

When I was about age ten, one day Anthony led me outside to the rear of his house and a large wooden storage box, the lid secured by a padlock. He opened it and within was the most amazing collection of sporting equipment.

Many kids had some sports gear—a baseball glove; a bat; maybe a football or basketball. Tony had at least six baseball gloves, numerous bats, baseballs, basketballs and footballs. He also had a complete catcher's gear outfit—mask, chest and leg protectors.

Looking at his treasure trove, I assumed we were gonna sample it. But he just shut and re-locked the lid. Strange, I thought. Why show me this great stuff if we're not gonna use it?

Equally strange was Anthony had all this gear but didn't participate in sports, organized or pickup. He almost seemed bored with his stash. I thought well, maybe another day.

But that day never came. And neither did his parents. He lived with his grandma. I didn't know why. His unused sports gear accumulation and his missing parents remained unsolved mysteries. And at that time, I didn't see how those two might have been related.

McGowan

Jimmy McGowan's nickname was "Scoop." Because he had scoops—new information that he loved to share. For example, in high school, he knew who were the easy teachers and maybe, easy girls. We took advantage of the teacher scoop, but the girl information was no help.

So yeah, Jimmy was newsworthy, but he wasn't trustworthy. How would we know if his scoops were real or just scoops of shit? His revelations were difficult to prove, and most were so obscure nobody cared if they were true or not. Like his insight into hot dog ingredients.

But one of his scoops was worthy of investigative verification. Late during senior year of high school, he told us about a bar that didn't card—the legal drinking age at that time and place was twenty-one—we were eighteen, or close.

The Blue Hen was no neighborhood dive. The Hen was a small nightclub with a house band. "Scoop's" scoop was to arrive early before the bouncer was on duty and the bartenders were purportedly known not to ask for an ID. You could drink and then stay for the music and likely avoid the cover charge.

So early one Friday evening, about 5 PM, Jimmy led five of us into the Blue Hen. We tried our best impersonation of six everyday guys casually sauntering into a watering hole to quench our thirst after a rough work week. Jimmy sat down on the first empty bar stool, and we single filed onto the adjoining stools.

The bartender came to Jimmy first. He ordered a Singapore sling. The bartender hesitated, stared at Jimmy, but finally nodded, and looked at the next guy. When the bartender didn't ask for Jimmy's ID, we followed his lead. Except nobody knew what Jimmy had just ordered, so lamely we each said same, same, same, same, same.

After the last kid ordered, the bartender stepped back and slowly scanned each of our faces. I thought well, it was a nice try, but now it was ID time. And I also thought why didn't Jimmy just order a beer? I mean, how often do six working stiffs belly up to a bar and start slamming Singapore slings?

I learned later that a Singapore sling contains many ingredients that require much preparation effort by the barkeep. Which probably explained the bartender telling us if we did this again, he'd card every one of us.

Dobrowski

Although most dogs frightened me, none of my customers did. Except for Mr. Alex Dobrowski. He was scary. It was nothing he ever did or ever said. He just looked frightening.

Mr. Dobrowski had slicked back hair, a pencil thin mustache, wore sharkskin razor cut creased suits, with a top pocket displayed handkerchief. His ensemble included silk ties secured to starched white shirts by gem-embedded tie clasps. A fedora hat and pointy Italian-style shoes bookended his ensemble package head to toe.

I was pretty sure he was mafioso, even though he wasn't Italian. My guess was he probably ran a Polish branch. But I found out from Mrs. Dobrowski that he was a home improvement salesman. Still, if I had an appointment to discuss home improvement and saw Mr. Dobrowski striding up my sidewalk, I would close all curtains, turn off all lights, lock all doors, and hide.

Now my fear of Mr. Dobrowski was likely unfounded paranoia, and he probably held no real threat to me, but I still took precautions. If I saw his car parked at the Dobrowski house, I skipped that collection stop. And I certainly was never foolish enough to include the Dobrowski's in my skipped paper rotation.

Rossi

Larry Rossi was a year older than me. Collecting one frigid January evening, I found Larry standing outside his house, without a coat and, strangely, wearing metal baseball spikes.

He then said to me, check this out. And he walked out onto the deserted dark street and started to jog down the ice-packed pavement. He stopped about three houses away, turned around, and began sprinting back. Running at full speed, as he came parallel to me, not breaking stride, he whistled, and his dog *Rooter* came tearing out from the side of his house, skidded a tad on the icy street before turning and racing after Larry.

Both disappeared into the darkness. When they returned, Larry wore a huge grin with Rooter in his arms. Now there is no real point to this brief story. Merely an embedded memory—a bitter, still, cold winter night—a boy and his dog happily having fun on an ice-packed, dark, empty urban street—and unknowingly creating a fond memory for me that I still retain.

PART 2
POST PAPER ROUTE

WISDOM

"If at first you don't succeed, destroy all evidence that you tried."

--Unknown

I brush my teeth every day. In fact, twice per day.

Certainly for hygienic reasons. But also because my best thinking occurs then. I'm aware that many people think deeply while showering. For me, the length and depth of my thoughts fits snuggly within the duration of my teeth cleansing.

During a recent brushing session, this tooth time thought emerged: I'm an old man now who has been around the block a few times since those four blocks on my paper route. Maybe it's time for me to give back. Share the wisdom gleamed from my lengthy life.

So I began to mentally peel the onion back on this wisdom sharing thought. But then I stopped peeling. Why peel an onion? A peeled onion is an unlikely source of wisdom. Wouldn't I just find more onion? And don't onions have enough on their plate keeping hamburgers and chili dogs appealing? Plus, just because onions make me cry, that's no excuse to peel off their skin. Onion lives matter.

My mental wisdom chase grew into a large glob of *wisdom sharing* Jello as it bounded down a steep rock-strewn hill. Trying to get my arms around it, eat it, and spit it out to you. Although that might be a crude analogy, I prefer to think of it as a micro-story.

As I mentally examined this further, I paused because beyond surviving to an elderly age, what useful wisdom did I actually have to share? Wisdom infers some aspect of success. But my success following my paper route has been elusive. And the primary contributor to my lack of success has been my challenge making decisions.

After going through several toothbrushes, a couple peeled onions, and some stints mentally chasing wisdom Jello down hills, I finally realized that what I really have to offer are a collection of thoughts, experiences, and stories about my decision making journey. Maybe some advice.

Then you can decide if anything that follows is helpful with your life decisions. Helpful either with how to do something or perhaps, how not to do it. It's your call if anything qualifies as wisdom. Because who am I to dictate to you what wisdom is? How rude.

DECISIONS

"Bad decisions make good stories."
--Ellis Vidler

I was born dehydrated. There was no documentation of the cause, but my theory is that when thrown into the deep end of Mom's birthing pool, I couldn't decide whether to float, play, sleep, eat, or drink.

That initial decision struggle has continued. Between the conclusion to my paperboy days and my current status as an old retired suburban guy, making decisions has been hard. With some poor results. Messy might be an accurate single-word summary of my post-paper route life. Four wives, fifty-eight jobs, and some homeless stints, brief I might add, are hints to my messiness.

Maybe it wouldn't be such a big deal if there weren't so many decisions to make. But they're everywhere. A non-stop continuous barrage that I find wearisome and annoying. I suppose I should just say what I'm thinking. Because truth must reign. Or is it rain? Or ring? Not sure, but regardless, I think decisions are a pain in the ass.

Like a functioning alcoholic, I'm a functioning ponderholic. I prefer to ponder rather than choose. Some might consider this procrastination. But that word has an ugly reputation, unfairly so in my mind.

Anyway, here's some of my thinking on basic decision-making.

Decidere, the original Latin word for decide, means "to cut off," as in slicing away alternative courses of action. Reducing the number of choices is beneficial, but has the downside of FOMO—fear of missing out—making a choice that might create regret for not choosing the other.

FOMO doesn't scare me. But FOFU does. Similar because both are capitalized four-letter acronyms starting with FO, FOFU is the fear of fucking up, a major contributor to my pondering.

Every decision has risk and potential regret. A few of my workarounds follow.

My favorite go-to is avoid the decision. Refuse to answer that decision door knock and ideally, the intruder goes away, taking that decision and potential regret bye-bye.

Another favorite is to outsource. Let someone else make the decision. If their choice doesn't work out, it's not my fault. I could and frequently do blame them for their poor choice.

When avoidance or outsourcing isn't an option, leaving me in the decision driver's seat, I go hybrid if available. Neapolitan ice cream is a good example. And I never choose Mahi-Mahi, a pathetic double down on potential regret.

Some of my choices are on automatic. I choose the same brand names for example. Not because they're better, but because they eliminate decisions and generally reduce surprises. Surprises are a regret carrier. So I go with the usual. Like Cheerios. They're reliable, and come with a little British flare, a small but nice bonus.

And not just brand names. Names in general have been a reliable approach. For my tree pruning needs, I always use Forrest. If I have a handy need, Handy Andy. For surgeries, it's only Dr. Cutter for me.

Experience has been helpful with similar decision situations. My experience with paper route dogs was helpful to my life-long decision to never own, feed, or pet a dog, avoiding death by dog meal.

Of course, the above doesn't cover all decision situations. When forced into a decision without a clue what's best, as a last resort, because it requires work, I might gather more information. There are several sources of information.

Other people can be information fountains. Jesus seems to be a frequent go-to guy. What would Jesus do? But I've hesitated to trust advice from the son of the top judge who gets indicted.

The media provides information. For simplicity, I choose information that agrees with what I already know and believe. Particularly conspiracy theories.

Another source of information is education. But more education doesn't guarantee improved decisions. Walker Percy said, "You can get straight A's but still flunk life." And Edith Pearlman says, "too much knowledge kills joy." I didn't want to flunk life or be a killjoy, so I've avoided this approach.

And does more information improve decisions? That seems logical. But that also assumes I decide logically. The reality is frequently I decide emotionally, then justify and defend the decision with logic.

For example, I might choose the rutabaga as a side dish for my entrée. I would choose rutabaga because it's a fun word to vocalize with few opportunities to say out loud. That emotional decision is then justified by the logic that Rutabaga is healthy.

Or here's a more interesting example. A friendship began because of our mutual enjoyment of red wine, a logical decision. Our relationship then grew romantic because of the sex, quite emotional. Or was it? Maybe the wine was emotional and the sex logical. Maybe both are logical. Or maybe both are emotional. Hmm. I'm in trouble here. My thought thread is unraveling. Boy, I can't believe how much better the pot is today than back in my day.

Concluding this decision analysis, my wishy-washy, namby-pamby tendencies will remain. I'm a loyal guy. I'll continue to just wing it. But once I pull a decision trigger, I don't change my mind. I am not a flip-flopper. Flip-flopping combined with wishy-washy and namby-pamby is not flattering. And suggests I might have some larger mental health issues, which happens to be the next topic I'll visit.

MENTAL HEALTH

"I'm sick of following my dreams. I'll just ask where they're going and hook up with 'em later."

--Mitch Hedberg

I'm normal. And I have documented proof.

I briefly lived in the town of Normal, where I met my first wife. She was from the tiny burg of Oblong. The *Oblong Observer* local newspaper announced our marriage: "Oblong Woman Marries Normal Man." That normal man specifically named me, Tom.

I always carry a shrunk, laminated copy of that in my wallet.

Although I'm documented normal, I do have a couple of harmless mental oddities I'll share for transparency.

I hear internal voices. Not continuously, they just pop in periodically, uninvited. But they're actually fun visitors. Sometimes we party. But if they get too rowdy, I just tell 'em to shut the fuck up.

Beyond FOFU, I also harbor a few other fears. Fear is the darkroom where negatives are developed. I found that in a fortune cookie—quite insightful, creatively composed, and from a credible source. Some consider fears irrational. That could be, but mine are rational to me.

Like my fear of dogs, which I've previously shared. But I also have a fear of horses, and by association, polo and rodeos. Everything about the equine world frightens me. Supposedly, familiarity can reduce fears. But I never saw a horse on my paper route. A few ponytailed girls were as close as it got. Now it's possible a Pinto might have hidden. I've heard they're notorious introverts.

Anyway, I thought the sole purpose for a horse is to be ridden. But on my only horse ride, with my naïve assumption I was in the driver's seat, the animal decided to be rid of my driver's ass, dumping that and the rest of my body onto the ground. My reaction was the expression pig-headed is a misnomer. Horse-headed is more accurate.

I stopped horsing around and retired, my decision grounded in the desire to stay grounded rather than get grounded, preventing forever the need to get off my high horse again.

Now I admit that I still like to watch old cowboy TV shows, *The Lone Ranger* a favorite. The Ranger sits comfy on Silver as his trusted horse goes through circus-type moves while the famous pre-pandemic masked man howls "hi-ho, hi-ho, off to work I go," and Tonto, nearby, shakes his head, embarrassed by the Kemosabe.

My self-assessment head scan identified those couple of quasi-abnormalities, which I've always just ignored. Then I thought, what the heck, why not get some professional feedback to reassure me I was mostly just a little weird. Maybe I get some help with my decision problems. Plus, I've always been curious if the rumors about psychiatrists' comfortable couches, and their magical drugs, were true.

So, I briefly-had a therapist, and we therapied. As far as I knew, he was a decent head guy, adept at hiding his yawns, and stifling his giggles.

Our session began with his question what were some of my life goals. Initially I drew a blank. But admitting I had no goals seemed to be the wrong way to establish my normalcy. So I replied my life goal was the pursuit of leisure.

His silent response confused me. Did it suggest either his disbelief or concern? Thankfully he then asked how he could help me. I shared with him my inner voices, fear of horses, and my decision challenges.

He quickly provided a deeper understanding of my horse fears. He told me horses weren't my issue. I was afraid of *large*.

Huh.

This insight became clearer to me during a deep trance on his comfy couch. A memory of my fourth birthday party emerged, and the huge balloon that mom gave me. The red, air-filled, circular thingy was several times larger than my head. The enormous size was scary enough, but when it abruptly, mysteriously, and loudly popped, I was petrified. And that fear has continued since that bizarre big balloon blew up. In fact, shortly after the incident, I briefly, and intentionally, stopped growing to prevent scaring myself.

My large fear has a clinical name—Largessesavitus—and it's a common condition. The esteemed mathematician, John Horton Conway, was a Largesseavitan. He not only faced his fear, he made it a career pursuit. He developed the Piano Problem: what is the largest object that can be maneuvered round a right-angled corner in a fixed-width corridor? And he also produced his "Monster Group"—a thing that exists in 196,883 dimensions.

As I considered my newly diagnosed large fear, I rationalized that it was quite rational, because large is both unnecessary and rarely successful. There is no benefit to large. History is full of examples of largesse failures—dinosaurs are kaput, dragons were slain, Jack's beanstalk was chopped down, Sears went bankrupt—all large, and largely short-lived. Conversely, small thrives. Ants for example.

Shrinky told me my inner voices, fear of large, lack of goals, and inability to make decisions were individually merely concerning. But collectively, he said, were abnormal. Which obviously generated some questions from me.

Are any of these life-threatening?
No.

Am I contagious?
No.

So, what's your point?
You're a sick man.

Says who?
Me. I'm your shrink. Remember?

OK. But don't beat around the bush doc. Give it to me straight.
You're mentally ill. Actually, you're pretty fucked up.

Oh, that's real professional. Pottymouth.
Well, I'm rubber, you're glue. What you say bounces off me and sticks on you.

Good one.
Thanks. It's an old-school playground classic.

That's when I produced my laminated mini-newspaper validation of my normalcy. The shrink poo-pooed my shrunk proof. He said it was a very early example of fake news.

Concluding our allotted session time, he told me he had suggestions for me to work on that would help me start to get my shit together.

Work on? Me? Really? That's when it became clear that he didn't know me. And I silently questioned if he cared about me. We obviously had serious compatibility issues.

So I shrank away from the shrink and never returned.

But what didn't shrink away was his comment about getting my shit together. It hung around until I decided to do something about it. I went to Office Depot.

While staring at file folders, Frank approached, and asked if he could help me. I told him I needed to get my shit together. He said follow me. And he led me to sticky notes.

Frank told me sticky notes are the start to getting my shit together. Great I said, but how do they work? He told me you capture sticky note moments onto a sticky note—stuff like random thoughts, recipe's, family names. But content, he said, isn't the point. What's important is you have written evidence you've started to get your shit together.

The sticky note section had several varieties and choices. Frank recommended traditional yellow, lined, 3 x 3 size. And he noted that because sticky notes are frequently lost, he suggested loading up with the shrink-wrapped multi-pack. And he also gave me a helpful tip for the lost sticky note problem—write a sticky note reminder where you put the sticky note. And then another sticky note reminder where you put your sticky note reminder.

I liked Frank's thinking. For a seventeen-year-old, he really seemed to have his shit together. He had more helpful input. Frank said although sticky notes stick, their purpose is temporary, a holding spot until the content is transferred onto a to-do list.

Frank told me to-do lists (TDL's) are neither new nor simple. There are three philosophical schools based upon the purpose, format, and content.

1. **Moses School**: Most think of Moses as a dapper-dressed, bearded, mountain-climbing holy man. But Moses was a TDL pioneer and retains a significant

current-day following. The Moses TDL serves purely to remind. Etched in stone, no item ever checked off, a religious zeal for stagnancy. The format is capitalized Roman Numeral, one through ten. Traditionally, Times New Roman font, but GenZ have toyed with *Papyrus*.

2. **Result School**: The Result sect is all about results. They employ a no-nonsense straight forward list format, items prioritized. Result TDL's are most dynamic—as tasks are completed, items are deleted with new items added.
3. **Process School**: Processors ignore results. They avoid any decision and keep all options open. Their TDL purpose is the creative process—the visual artistic journey—format, font style, size, color. Items are organized by numbers, letters, alphabetical, and bullets. Priority listing is rare.

It was clear to me I have Process tendencies. Their vision philosophically aligns closer to my leisure vision. List construction is pleasurable without the messy details of doing anything—an opportunity to disguise dysfunctionality. I'm strongly leaning in that direction.

So far I've purchased the shrink wrapped multipack sticky notes. But haven't pulled the trigger on incorporation nor decided upon a TDL strategy. I'm currently in pondering mode.

PHYSICAL HEALTH

"My daily workout is jumping to conclusions, running late, and dodging adult responsibilities."
--Unknown

Although paying attention to physical health makes sense, the benefit of poor health is increased couch time, a compelling leisure activity. But maybe you should ignore that.

I'm gonna dig right into my physical health thoughts by digging into food.

I've always been a picky eater. I pick foods that taste good. My paper route gave me the freedom to pick those tasty foods without an adult "eat your peas" supervision.

Saturday's, after the morning paper delivery, and having concluded my payment business at the paper office, I was starving. So I began to explore the many downtown food offerings. After some experimentation, I settled into an efficient walking buffet culinary circuit.

One of my first discoveries was *Veronica's Bakery*. Upon entry, the aroma of warm freshly baked bread and pastries was heavenly. I was silently greeted by several white-haired, white-floured, white-aproned, white ladies. They stared and smiled down at my ten-year-old tiny presence from behind their L-shaped display counters.

They made me uncomfortable. I felt they exuded a lack of respect I deserved as a businessman who had just minutes previously conducted an important financial transaction.

Because of my discomfort, and the abundance of choices, I didn't dilly or dally. I quickly ordered a glazed donut. The ladies hesitated, suggesting their own discomfort, probably wondering where's mom? Show us the money. When I did show them the money that first time, and every Saturday morning for over six years, our mutual discomfort went away.

It was a delicious donut. And tasted better without Mom reminding me to chew slowly with my mouth closed. The pastry found its way into my stomach within three steps out the door.

The donut was just an appetizer to take my hunger edge off. It was a short walk to the *Hamburger Sop*. The actual name was the *Hamburger Shop*, but the "h" portion of the neon sign was defective. The Sop was an old train dining car without the train, minus the railroad tracks. I wondered if the car became permanently stationary because it got lost or had been derailed.

In addition to the broken signage, the interior was equally artistic. No tacky tables. Just a classy counter with circular cracked vinyl swivel seats for about twelve self-seating people. But I wasn't there for the elegant ambiance. Or a hamburger. I was there for their great chili dogs. There's just something special about a morning chili dog to coat the stomach for the day.

Then I walked down to *Neds* for a snack. *Ned's* was a hole in the wall; no seating, just a small standing window counter. A White Castle protégé, the entire menu were tiny rectangular burger sliders, served with fried onions. On my first visit, I learned that fried onions were mandatory. I told Ned no onions. Ned said onions. I said no. He said yes. I said no. Guess what he said? And guess who won? I ate the onions.

The next culinary buffet stop was at Kramer's Hardware store for some hot, buttered, salted popcorn. Self-served. And free. Not sure why the hardware store offered free popcorn, but I didn't want to question free. The popped corn I considered an additional vegetable to the fried onions for some healthy balance to my diet.

My concluding energy intake was dessert at *Logners*, conveniently located at my bus stop corner. *Logners* was a multi-floored ancient department store. It was dimly lit with uneven wooden floors that creaked; the overhead fans squeaked. The store sold things piled haphazardly upon rectangular tables. Based upon the dust, some of the stuff might have been original inventory from the 1800's store opening, waiting for the right buyer, which certainly wasn't me.

Because I wasn't there to shop. I was there to eat. Seated upon a stool at the lengthy counter, I always ate a sundae—vanilla ice cream, thick hot fudge sauce, nuts, whipped cream, and cherry topped—served in a tall glassware, with a long thin spoon perfectly designed to remove all contents.

It's unlikely my downtown walking buffet provided you with any food for thought. But Victor Lindlahr's book, *You Are What You Eat*, might give you something to chew on.

Victor says our food is converted into our hair, eyes, nose, mouth, lungs, fingernails, and many other body tissues. He seems to provide compelling logic to eat good stuff. But what I wonder is aren't those body parts already in place *before* I dine? Doesn't it seem a little late to think what I eat will have any further beneficial impact?

And his suggestion to watch what we eat raised another question. My body is an enclosed temple. Once food gets past my lip gates, it disappears, so how do I watch it? I suppose a food mirror might help. But isn't it rude to chew with an open mouth?

My guess is once my food has entered, I can only pray it works out. And if true, I wonder if that's how the tradition of saying grace before meals started.

***

My walking food buffet choices may have been a questionable healthy habit, but the walking part had to be a good healthy habit that I retain today.

Now at one point I was actually a jogger. I ran outdoors. Connecting with nature. And outside also allowed me to smoke as I ran. The downside to exterior participation is the terrains are uneven, the weather unpredictable, and the experience is lonely.

Those variables prompted me to take my running inside to a health club. The indoor track was flat, weatherproofed, and it helped reduce my smoking. The club also provided me the social aspect I craved, with a support group of health-conscious peers.

Ultimately, I adjusted my jogging. I found jogging tiresome, very non-leisure, and sweaty. I slowed it down to a saunter, and then to a fast walk. Then to a slow walk. So slow, that now as I walk laps, most of my shared oval space comrades pass me. As a passing thought, actually all but two whisk by.

One who didn't pass me was *Really Old Guy*. He had to be at least 97. He ate my dust. And I also left *Rehab Man* in my wake. He wore a neck to ankle body brace. I was tempted to say to each of them to pick it up a bit buddy as I flew by them. But I didn't. Although I love the social aspect of walking, I've never actually spoken with anyone. It's hard to chat with moving people. Some chairs might help.

The only person I had an interaction with was *Multitasker*. She walked into my life when she walked into me while she was reading a book. I had no idea book reading walkers were so aggressive. Seems like they should take their walking to the library. Anyway, when she stopped after our collision, I expected her to apologize.

But instead, she told me to pick up my pace.

I've recently tweaked my ambling routine. Walking is time intensive and more so at my snail pace. So my walk-around time-saving alteration was to start my ambles at 11:55 PM and conclude at 12:05 AM., delivering an efficient two days in a row workout.

***

Sex is a physical health topic. I think. Experts recommend specific exercises to improve sexual performance and enjoyment. I've delayed incorporating this into my life. Not because I dispute the advice. It just seems to me I should first find a sexual partner before I work on sexual improvement.

***

Sleep might be my favorite health activity. And shut eye is critical for a balanced leisure life. Leisure can be exhausting. One of my early hero's was Rip Van-something or other—the old guy with the impressive beard. That man could flat out rip some Z's.

Luckily, sleep comes easy for me, but not everyone. I realize that some must work at it. But if sleep requires work, it seems logical to do it at work. In addition to work naps, other siesta opportunities include church services—a little nod to the sleep gods—at school, and maybe during some spousal conversations.

***

Health experts recommend many glasses of water daily. I not only concur, as a supplement, I drink several beers daily. The downside to my beer supplement is an upside to my stomach. I have a beer belly. With all of the attention on health, it's surprising we have yet to discover a cure.

***

I previously shared, quasi-bragged, about my teeth brushing diligence. One reason for my teeth maintenance focus that I failed to mention was my desire to avoid the dentist.

As medical knowledge and technology leaps forward, the dental profession seems to remain stuck somewhere in the mid-sixth century. Teeth are still ripped out with pliers and any remnants hacked out with a saw.

OK, I admit I'm a dental-phobic. It's both embarrassing and a tad surprising given how smooth my first dental visit went. Mom took me and one of my younger sisters. As the oldest and a big boy, Mom had me go first to show little sis there was nothing to fear.

So, I stepped up into my leadership role and bounded fear free into the dental arena where I did male bravado proud, my performance rewarded with a red "badge of courage" sucker.

The "me first" plan sorta worked—except my influence on my baby sister was overrated. She went in screaming. I could hear the battle cries. But when she emerged from the war theater, she was also given a red sucker. Her award was not warranted; totally unfair. But I was partially comforted knowing she couldn't have possibly enjoyed her unearned prize.

As an adult, I somehow managed to slip into an unplanned, twenty-one-year dentist visit absence. And as time passed, a dread emerged. Then the dread grew into fear, panic, and phobia. Any aspect of dentistry was taboo. At my degenerative depths, I stopped yawning.

But for some reason, I was unable to avoid periodic dental dreams. One was a recurring nightmare. I lay prone upon a nearly horizontal dental chair, peering up at strain-faced tooth personnel. My mouth was opened to inhuman dimensions, secured with dental clamps.

The professionals were desperately attempting to retrieve sharp instruments that had mistakenly fallen down my throat. A blood lake begins to fill my reservoir and teeth float atop the crimson pool. I hear *code blue. Repeat. We have code blue.*

Their taut faces then fade to calm, gazing at me in my casket, a red sucker propped into my folded hands.

If you're wondering, yes, I did return to the dentist. At age 46. Mom took me.

***

My annual physical is with Ponytail Doctor. I'm not a manbun fan, but older men with ponytails imply confidence, a trait I like with doctors, particularly surgeons. Anyway, he's quite good, magical with his toy hammer.

Following my exam, we usually walk outside for a smoke and he always tells me I should stop smoking. I always ask why. He always says so I won't die. I always ask if I stop, will I never die? He always says no, I'll just live longer.

Living longer seems to be the universal medical community goal—to extend life. But I'm not sure I will want an extension if my prolonged life is a fucked-up existence. What I think I want in the end from a medical intervention is their best drugs.

But I also realize this may not be my final decision. It's possible if I'm diagnosed with some deadly malady, I will toss that thinking, do a one-eighty flip, and tell them to do all and any interventions available to keep my ass alive. I know I've earlier disparaged flip-flopping, but now I'm saying there might be exceptions.

Recently, my prostate PSA (I think it means *Puffy Stuff Abnormality*) numbers were outside normal. The prostate is some thingy inside mostly male butts. I know what you're thinking. Not another old guy prostate story. But this one's different. It's my prostate.

I think bad medical news generates one of three approaches:

1. Ignore it and hope it goes away.
2. Take some drugs and hope it goes away.
3. Aggressive intervention with chemo, radiation, or surgically gouge the damn thing out. I think part of the knife strategy is a hope the word spreads internally to other body parts to do their job or meet the same fate.

Ponytail Doctor recommended I consult a urologist. I'm OK with consulting.

While seated in the exam room, a kid about twelve years old entered. I assumed he was there to empty the trash. But as you probably guessed, he was the urologist.

He asked me to drop my pants so he could peek. A little forward I thought for a first consulting date. He ignored me when I said you first. Anyway, peeking sounded harmless. But his *take a peek* went to extremes. He shoved something up my butt. That roadway has always been one-way. And opposite of his direction.

After I retrieved my clothing and a little bit of my dignity, my young urologist told me my prostate was large. I thanked him for noticing. He then suggested I should have an MRI.

There are no results yet as I write this. But if you'd like an update, send me an email.

I think that covers my ass and my body, a thoughtful courtesy all old guys should heed.

MONEY

"Do you know why dogs have no money? No pockets."
--Jerry Seinfeld

Can money buy happiness? Collective wisdom suggests not. But I would have volunteered to test the theory. More money may not have turned me serially giddy, but I suspect it would have increased my smiles.

I've often wondered what if the question were flipped. Can happiness buy money? Now wouldn't that be nice? But would it? Would it be easier to achieve happy or money? Happiness or moneyness?

That's probably enough philosophical exploration.

My paper route was the peak of my financial journey. Without verifiable proof, I'm pretty sure I was in the top 1% of all 10-year-old money earners globally. And I don't think that's an example of the older I get the better I was.

Since then, I've struggled to accumulate financial wealth. For two reasons.

The first is bad luck. Which seems to be a recurring theme to my general lack of success. The plethora of potential windfall money sources have eluded me. Inheritance for example. It didn't have to be crazy huge. I have a minimalist lifestyle. Just a little jump start to get me on my feet. Even a mil or two could have taken the edge off my money stress.

So would an insurance beneficiary payout. Or winning the lottery, or an early play on the Tesla stock. Maybe a little more realistic, luck at the gaming tables or picking a long shot at the dog track. Which reminds me of how I once placed a bet on a dog that started the race but never finished. My dog was smaller than the other entrants. Never proven, but I think my dog was mistaken for an energy bar and eaten mid-race, not surprising in this dog-eat-dog world.

When I asked the cashier for a refund, she sent me to lost and found. But they were no help. On a positive note, thankfully the adage the less you bet, the more you lose when you finally win didn't apply in that case.

Getting back on track, off the track, my employment track record is the second reason for my money woes.

The paper route was my longest employment tenure and one of the few stints that didn't end with my dismissal. Following that wealthy paper route heyday, I've had many jobs. And when I say many, I mean a lot, assuming fifty-eight qualifies as both many and a lot.

The jobs I secured were ones with an urgent employer need for a warm body to do unpleasant tasks that required no skill, good fits for me. The only thing I brought was laziness.

And obviously those were poor paying jobs that resulted in my weak financial accumulation.

***

But enough about my money moves. I actually have a couple money generating ideas that are too late for me but maybe not you. They're non-traditional money paths whose core concepts are valid, serve a need and be lucrative.

Try this. Establish a 24/7, worldwide, 1-800-ART-HELP resource for artist assistance.

Let me expand. Artists frequently hit a creative wall. They get stuck. A lull in their creative creations, lulls that can be lengthy, and time is money. Your help desk would provide instant help. Here are a couple of applicable historical examples.

Writer's block is most common. Charles Dickens for example. Chuck was stuck on his opening line: It was kind of good times with some bad times. He felt it was an awkward start, but it took him years to tweak *it was the best of times and the worst of times.*

Musicians end up in lyrical dead ends. Tony Bennet thought he forgot his heart in Sacramento. After a lengthy delay, a cousin finally suggested he may have left it in San Francisco. Dylan took forever to replace *like a tumbling rock* with *like a rolling stone.*

Painters paint themselves into corners. Like Michelangelo. Mike was mired in canvas mud all over the floor. After a long pause, by pure luck, he happened to look up at the dreary Sistine Chapel ceiling. That led to a chapel ceiling niche with soaring success. With your help, it wouldn't have taken him that long.

Sculptors are prone to block issues. The sculptor brothers, Hank and Randy Block, are a famous example. Their blockness reached such depths they accepted the suggestion to move to Texas for inspiration. But rather than Texas, they mistakenly heard *taxes.* They stopped sculpting, created H & R Block, a financial success. But at what cost? Your artist resource might have saved the world two world-class sculptors.

***

My second idea. Like cowbells, can we ever have too many apps? And anyone can develop one. I think the best app opportunity is in technology. And more so if the tech app could interface with our anatomy to improve our body.

Have you ever noticed we have ten toes? Are all ten necessary? Our little toe has always been functionally suspect. The Pluto of the toe universe seems to have no purpose. How about an app that finds a use for the little piggy?

Here's how it might work. A software chip is surgically inserted into our brain, then linked to hardware—a tiny multiplexer, a teeny router, a minute preamp, and micro-Yagi directional antenna. This infrastructure transmits the app signal via Bluetooth to a mini receiver implanted into the wee-wee.

This would provide total control of the minor foot member, including potentially altering its physical characteristics. Like changing its length, width, and maybe firmness.

The final piece to this implementation puzzle is to figure out how a longer, thicker, stiffer baby toe appendage might improve its function. I'm not sure because I'm more of a big picture, big idea, big toe guy. But that wrinkle can be ironed out. Likely before lunch. I mean launch.

***

I think retro contrarianism has wealth opportunity. The idea is a little unorthodox, but identify current trendy thinking, then go the other way. When everyone abandons something, perhaps that's the time to jump in and go retro before retro goes retro. Think vinyl records.

Here's the concept. Paperboys are extinct. In part, because analog print newspapers became untrendy, replaced by trendier online digital news sources. Clichés are similarly out of vogue, widely disdained.

How are these related? Start a print newspaper and then own the cliché niche.

Let's run this up the flagpole and see how to kill two birds with one stone.

It's no secret the printed word is going down the drain. And clichés are hanging by a thread. But if you merged the print world with the cliché world might both be saved?

To get the ball rolling, let's examine for posterity, clichés.

A chip off the old block, clichés were a perfectly descriptive little collection of words. And cute. They were our darlings. But then, familiarity bred contempt, the corner was turned, love turned to scorn, then down the slippery slope to hate. Cliché's became losers. Who loves a loser?

But are these word gangs a terrorist threat to the mother tongue? Are they bad wordies? Undesirable syllabic mongrels not to be uttered, even by cows? I think not. Clichés are seasoned veterans and can be a sight for sore eyes.

Right, wrong, or indifferent, and you may beg to differ, but with all due respect, don't look this gift horse in the mouth just because it's one of a different color.

And print newspapers? Concern abounds, digital is snapping at printed newspaper heels. But a real paper is one in the hand and perhaps worth two in the bush. Press those print presses back into service and beyond a shadow of a doubt your readers will begin to see the forest for the trees and will stick with you through thick and thin. And it's better than even money you could find a fortune in small change.

Print has stood the test of time, a point well taken. So, raise the roof and lower the boom on digital pretentiousness and become a solid as a rock reader resource.

On the other hand, this half-baked idea may not be the best since sliced bread. It could backfire as the oldest trick in the book, sending your print world to hell with all your eggs in one hand basket, teaching you a lesson to be learned. This fight to the finish may get you caught red handed if readers view clichés as the root of all evil, knowing one when they see one.

But that has little to no chance if you pour your heart and soul into the heart of the matter. You're at the right place at the right time to stand up and be counted.

However, this is no place for the faint-hearted. And don't be stubborn as a mule. Trust me on this, the bottom line is if you don't allow those digital dogs their day, throw them a bone, teach them a new trick, or let 'em bark up your tree, they could be left high and dry.

Will this save our *Daily Planet*? Too late. But Clark, Lois, Perry, and Jimmy will roll over in their graves, be pleased as punch, and respect you in the morning when you practice what you preach in print and deal those online black sheep news wannabes' a knockout blow before they know what hit them.

In conclusion, this is where the rubber meets the road. I rest my case, giving a wakeup call and lending a helping hand. Think outside the box.

And you can print that.

***

While I'm in the retro vein, whatever happened to prospecting as a career? I just never hear about the profession anymore. Was getting hands dirty the demise? But that doesn't make sense. Playing in dirt has romantic appeal, as portrayed in old TV Westerns.

Those films usually opened with a solitary, bearded, sweat-stained hatted, pick-in-hand, old guy mining a gold nugget. He places his mined find into his string-tied bag hidden behind a rock. Then a bad guy shows up. They sit around the campfire, eat beans, and share a half pint, then go to sleep.

Except the bad guy fakes sleep. He finds the gold bag, and sneaks off with the loot, pack mule and water canteen. We think the old timer is fucked. But then a good guy arrives, tracks down the bad guy, returns the old timer's pack mule, canteen and gold bag, and the old guy lives happily ever after.

If digging, eating beans, and sleeping on the ground is appealing, a prospecting career should appeal. But realistically, is prospecting a realistic option? It's hard work.

Hats don't get sweat stained on their own. And I'm starting to wonder how realistic those movies were.

***

I've delayed this long enough. If, like me, you have no aspirations or skills, go into sales.

Believe it or not, we are all natural salespeople, as Daniel Pink explains in his book, *To Sell Is Human.* But it's interesting that, as little kids, when adults seeking humor asked us what we wanted to be when we grew up, in the history of this tradition, sales has never been cited.

Nobody chooses sales. All salespeople, myself included, accidentally stumble into the job as a last resort. But with my depth and breadth of sales experience, let me share some helpful professional insights.

Within the sales arena are many choices. For starters, avoid selling to consumers. They're a pain in the ass. Largely because they're spending their own money. Sell to business or, even better, government buyers. They have play money.

Next, try to sell for a large, deep pockets company. They are more likely to provide generous expense accounts. Ideally, the big company is headquartered far away from your sales territory. That would increase the odds that nobody at corporate would know that the Red Door location of your sales meeting wasn't a restaurant, it was a strip club.

But large organizations do have downsides. They tend to have more meetings that are long, boring, rambling verbal assaults, absent linguistic rights-of-way. There's never a verbal cop when you need one. If possible, don't participate.

***

Every job has a boss. Most are challenging quirky headcases. Particularly sales bosses. One example should suffice.

He was a retired Marine with combat experience and some residual post-war mental health damage. Exhibited by his extreme passion for team building activities. These activities were really disguised survival training. He seemed to confuse our sales team with a military squadron. But his sales troops were fat, urban, fifty-something old guys. Our only survival experience was not falling off outdoor tavern decks.

The first year he trudged us off to the mountains for white water rafting. We had envisioned sliding down a curved plastic tube at a waterpark. But instead, we entered atop an actual river before entering below it. Then there was the scuba diving adventure. I'll spare you the details of that disaster. He was in final preparations for our next team building event, sky diving into a remote Southeast Asian jungle, when the boss suddenly died. Tragic, but he really left us no choice.

Speaking of bosses, I wouldn't recommend becoming one. I've never been one myself, nor even been considered. But should you have that opportunity, keep Casey Stengel's insight in mind. When the former famous Yankees baseball manager was asked what was the secret to his long manager success, he said he always kept those who hated him away from those undecided.

My final money/work heads-up is a tip from Steven Wright. He advises never work at a fire hydrant factory. You won't be able to park anywhere near the place.

I wish you the best with your money chasing decisions as I move on to a different place.

PLACE

"My grandmother started walking five miles a day when she was 60. She's 97 today and we don't know where the hell she is."

--Ellen DeGeneres

My twenty-eighth birthday snuck up on me. I wasn't prepared.

Mom had established the Rule of 28, the final age she allowed us kids to live at home. She apparently felt the need to establish the rule or she would never achieve emptynestness.

It was very intuitive of her based upon me. Because it was likely I may not have left on my own. Remember FOMO-fear of missing out? There is a lesser-known meaning—fear of moving out. My fear was driven by the simple fact I had no clue where to go.

So, I walked over to Mark Grassley's. As a reminder, Mark was my paper route friend with whom I played nerf hoops and wiffle ball. And we still continued to play. Mark remained living at his parents' house because they had yet to establish a kick out rule.

But he was starting to get some hints which prompted his research into that likely future. He discovered a book by Chuck Pettis, *Secrets of Sacred Space*. One of the secrets was Catholic Churches were frequently open 24/7, providing the opportunity to extend a visit beyond spiritual needs. The Holy Water fonts offered a thirst quench as well as a sponge bath. For a snack, the heavenly host wafer was available at every Mass.

He suggested I check out St. Mary's for my possible brief habitat.

I was initially excited about this convenient solution. The church was less than two blocks away. But then I remembered and reminded Mark that Father George was still there. And the pastor still didn't allow hanging outside in the church alley for smoking and drinking club meetings. What's the chance he'd let me hang inside his holy space?

But that alley reflection triggered another alley thought. The alley behind the newspaper building where the wino Gooseneck lived.

And that's where I went. Remarkably, Gooseneck still lived there. When I set up house with my sleeping bag, Gooseneck didn't welcome me warmly. He emitted a cool, aloof vibe that I dismissed as probably standard alley host demeanor.

But when I brought him a bottle of cheap wine as an alley warming gift, he softened. And when I reminded him that I had contributed money to him but no verbal abuse for 6 years as a former paperboy, he invited me into his new home, a large dumpster.

I loved what he had done with the place. He had really gotten his shit together.

He told me he continued his Saturday morning theatrical performances in his dirty clothing and the paperboys continued to give him money, but their verbal taunts had waned since his dumpster upgrade. His initial cool reception to my presence he admitted, was a concern I would be a competitor and take a bite out of his paperboy sales target market.

I assured him my residence was temporary and no threat to his alley begging monopoly. Gooseneck was also worried the alley was starting to get gentrified. Could be I told him but he could relax that I was not any sort of trend setting leader.

***

After settling into my new alley habitat, I began to seriously contemplate getting my shit together. Come up with a game plan for a more permanent place to live. Thankfully, I didn't have to start at the very beginning of my planning process. Someone had already chosen my universe, planet, continent, and country. I appreciated whomever made those choices.

Initially I gave thought to rural accommodations, thinking there were likely some inexpensive living arrangements in the boonies. Although I had always lived in this country, I had never lived in the country. Scanning my limited awareness of rural life, barn hay lofts held a certain cozy, rustic, romantic appeal. And caves seemed worthy to explore until I learned of the dangers of spelunker gangs.

But who was I kidding? I wasn't gonna be a country boy. I was a city guy.

***

I won't go through my subsequent living space trials and errors. I ultimately ended up in Minnesota. A good choice. Wish I could claim it as mine. But it was a wife's job move.

Minnesota is a little strange, not a bad fit for me. Here is the roots of Dylan, Prince, and My Pillow Guy. And home of the world's largest ball of twine. (In Darwin. Twelve-foot circumference, 17,400 pounds. Francis Johnson rolled the twine 4 hours daily for 29 years.)

Many Scandinavians reside here. They're weird even within this weird place. But I respect their embrace of leisure. They love to fish, ski, hot tub, and drink. And are really into hunting. When I was told the state bird was the mosquito, I assumed that was just goofy Norwegian humor. Not so. There's a mosquito hunting season, bow only. Uffda.

Although it has a reputation as a cold place, I've found it to be warm—the warmth of *Minnesota Nice* people. There are nice people everywhere. But Minnesota nice is extreme. Early on I arrived at a four-way stop simultaneously with cars at the other three stop signs. We were there for seven minutes, nicely waiting for the other person to go first. Minnesota Nice seems to include an aversion to being first so others won't feel like losers.

Which explains why their professional sports teams have not only not won championships, they actively avoided winning. The Vikings football team have lost four Super Bowls, supposedly intentionally. The North Stars hockey team came so embarrassingly close to winning the Stanley Cup they snuck out of town, permanently moving to Dallas.

Those examples I suppose seem plausible. But this next one is a real stretch. Former Minnesota Senator Hubert Humphrey was LBJ's VP and 1968 Democratic presidential nominee. Humphrey was leading Richard Nixon, his Republican candidate foe, late in the election. Apparently, on the verge of victory, Humphrey became nervous with his potential win that he started to campaign for Nixon. The reason this might be true is there's no other explanation for anyone losing to Nixon.

***

Ultimately it's nice to find a place and establish firm roots. Where we can lay our heads every evening. The final place frontier. The choice of a specific space place of community.

This decision might be dictated by a job. If not, the choice depends upon what's important. If big is desirable, go to the suburbs. Suburbia has big streets, big houses, big yards, big garages, big stores with big numbers of choices to buy stuff, and quickly eat stuff.

Suburbia is the American Dream. The showcase of what we do best—sell stuff and feed each other. I reflect upon our good fortune to be living in America today. Not too long ago, every community offered an endless array of mom-and-pop retailers. A relentless string of potential unreliability. You never knew what you would get at those places.

But suburbia is where the real pros fixed that. The national retailer boys knew their stuff. They removed any potential unpleasant surprises. Sameness was perfected. A replica experience guaranteed. And they made it easy for us to get to their stuff. They really know parking, providing sprawling blacktop parking lots, eliminating the need to search for a car space and removed the annoying nuisance and challenge of parallel parking.

And when I say the national pros are here, I'm not talking about some of them. Every national chain arrived to help us buy the plethora of national stuff. Target, Walmart, Penny's, Costco, Walgreen's, CVS, Home Depot, and Menards is a small sample.

As impressive as that list is, (I won't get into any further discussion of stuff. Stuff is our next topic), the foodies take our efficient eat needs to another level.

Some examples of eatery presence include Burger King, White Castle, Perkins, Hardee's, Jack-in-the-Box, Krystal, Culver, Sonic, Arby's, Houlihan's, McDonald's, KFC, Chick-Fil-A, Popeye's, Domino's, Pizza Hut, Old Chicago.

And for some female diversity, Wendy's.

I'm not sure why I bothered to itemize all those names. They're common knowledge. Plus, I'm not a suburban knowledge guru. Because I'm not a suburban guy. That's not who I am. It's just where I live. It's where I sleep. But it's not where I dream.

When my pillow does its job, I drift back walking through a neighborhood on narrow streets with small houses on small yards, past people I know and they me. Trekking onward to the laundromat for some deep thinking and into smoke filled Andy's Tap. Where Frankie, Mr. Chang, and Father McMurphy are. Where only good friends can playfully call each other Wop, Spic, Pollock, Chink.

And I take bus rides with crabby drivers through other neighborhoods to Gooseneck's alley, Veronica's Bakery, Hamburger Sop, Ned's, Kramer's Hardware, Logner's Department Store.

Suburbia might be the American dream. But it's not my dream.

STUFF

"You can't have it all. Where would you put it?"
--Steven Wright

Americans have an innate need to acquire stuff. Some necessary, much questionable.

I doubt if many people consider themselves hoarders. Those with accumulation challenges are more likely to consider their stuff collections or some other favorable descriptor.

My family dabbled in collecting. Dad collected jobs. Mom, empty wine bottles. Not so sure about my siblings. But my brothers seemed to hang on to swear words and lies. My sisters had a lot of bobby pins. That last one might be sexist, but I don't think so.

The Romano's, my crossword-saving paper customer, were also collectors.

Myself? I'm a minimalist. It requires discipline to restrain my acquisition urges. My minimalist discipline was made easier with my minimalist money. And another reason I don't accumulate stuff is the more items I have, the harder it is to keep track of them.

I frequently forget where I put something, and some of those somethings move from misplaced to lost. The only pets I've ever had have been peeves. One pet peeve is when I can't find what I need. My response to the missing or lost is not pretty.

A missing sock is a recurring peever. I usually don't look for it, I just hope it shows up. But one day I was so annoyed with a lost sock, I decided to try and track it down. I began my search at the most likely place it might be hiding, the laundry room. Between the stacked washer/dryer and the wall was a narrow space. I think that space might be called a kit and kaboodle. But that doesn't sound right. No, I think it's a nook and cranny, a more inviting hideout for a reticent sock.

My exploration of the nook's cranny uncovered an assortment of stuff—four pennies, a golf ball, the Monopoly deed to St. Charles Place, a pair of women's panties, a WD40 tiny red wand, expansion foam, a dusty can of Endust, and one yellow, elbow-length rubber glove. And shockingly, there it was, the sock.

I retrieved the foot cover, but I left behind the other items. They weren't mine. But I did take the women's panties. Although they weren't mine and not my color, they looked good on me, so finders' keepers.

***

Even if we aren't hoarders, once we have something, it can be tough to get rid of it. Although I don't have a lot of stuff, I have found it difficult to de-have it. My delete decisions have sometimes been a challenge.

The easiest way to reduce my questionable retentions is to just toss them. That solution is easier to do with other people's garbage, but our valuables create hesitation. My rid struggles are classic examples of FOMO (fear of missing out) and FOFU (fear of fucking up).

I still regret throwing away that naked picture of my old girlfriend. Lesson learned. So, I gave pause to pitching my five-year paperboy service award plaque. It was a stunning work of art, crafted from a time when plaques were plaques.

As challenging as that decision was, a more difficult lose it dilemma was my 6th grade *Free Throw Contest* trophy. This was no trivial participation award. This was a serious piece of documented success. My name and second place professionally etched upon a metal plate screwed into a real wood base, supporting a life-like miniature hoopster, two hands on the ball, both extended skyward to a full seven inches.

A shame you never saw it. It was truly impressive. So much so that a visitor once exclaimed, *wow, no idea you were such an accomplished roundballer.* I humbly replied *well, what can I say?* My effort at generating a blush was unsuccessful.

I finally decided it was time to pitch both. I mean, was I really that insecure I needed to keep those reminders of my successes? Yes. Anyway, after lugging the trophy and plaque around for over a half century, I finally threw them into the garbage.

But this was not a hasty impromptu throw away act. After 50 years of contemplation, I decided to duct tape them together. My thought was that their future garbage dump discovery by archeologists would trigger further research into who this incredibly successful person was, culminating in my lasting personal legacy. Granted, it's a long shot, beyond free throw length, but my best shot.

***

What I should have done with the plaque and trophy was recycle them. But going green was a lifestyle change that took me a while to adopt. I started with food container jars and cans, a seemingly easy adjustment from just tossing them in the garbage. But nothing is easy.

First, the food in the jars and cans had to be thoroughly emptied. Peanut butter jars can never be totally peanut butter gone. And the cream of soups—mushroom, chicken, tomato—are a bitch to de-soup. So, I found it easier to just stop buying any food that doesn't slide easily and completely from the container. Canned corn and green beans have become a staple. Those foods exit with no trace of visiting.

Another struggle with managing discards is the stuff that doesn't fit in the recycling container. Like my pair of old, bald, car tires. My solution for those used rubbers was to send them rolling down the street on a dark, cloudy night. I'm not proud of that, but it was successful. And might you agree the solution was kinda creative?

***

An alternative to either pitching or recycling stuff is to repurpose it. Find a new use for the useless thing. As I did with my truck bumper, a detail warranting more detail.

One day I saw in my backyard a small piece of metal on the ground. When I stooped down to pick it up, it didn't budge. Digging with a shovel I ultimately found that the miniature metal was attached to a humongous buried truck bumper. When the monster was finally extracted, it was a tad rusted, but still functional. A real keeper. And if I had a truck, useful as a backup bumper if my truck bumper got bumped off. Hmmm.

I briefly considered purchasing a truck but abandoned the idea. And I realized I should just get rid of *Bumper.* Yes, I named it. I had become emotionally attached. I mean, how often does an orphaned truck bumper just show up? Might this be some sort of an omen?

Anyway, I wasn't sure what to do with *Bumper.* I thought that maybe the humanitarian thing to do was release it back into its natural habitat buried in the ground. Let it live out its final 263,472 years on this earth. Or I suppose in rather than on this earth. Then I donned my slightly dusty thinking cap. What have others done with their spare truck bumpers? That thought thread ultimately led me to the Deep South, where defunct appliances are converted into yard art. What Yanks bury, Rebs display.

So, I bumped *Bumper* onto the front porch and repurposed it as porch art. But porch art appreciation is not universal. Wife #3 was not initially impressed. But when the neighbors' compliments began? Well, that still didn't change her opinion.

But the requests for truck bumpers began to roll in. And I've since made three porch art buying trips to southern Georgia. No luck with truck bumpers, but I have picked up a few refrigerators and stoves.

***

Minimalist or not, there's some stuff I need. And some need to be replaced. Here again is where restraint is necessary. A helpful tool is a shopping list and only buy what is on the list.

But when my only need was to replace toothpaste, a list was unnecessary. I went to Target. I always choose Target because they have everything. Plus, I know how to get there. Upon entry, I ignored the variety of shopping containers. This was a one and done, in and out.

But on my way to toothpaste, I saw a $1 coupon attached to a large bag of cotton balls. An unexpected bonanza. Not sure about you, but I go through a lot of cotton balls. I grabbed 'em.

Onward toward teeth maintenance, there was a BOGO AA battery offer. An appealing, compelling opportunity. Not something to flippantly dismiss. Batteries are sneaky, slipping past freshness dates. Ever Readies are never ready. I nabbed them.

After returning to the front for a hand basket, I found the toothpaste. And a Buy 3 Get 1 Free shrink-wrapped pack.

Hmm… must I buy 3 three-some's to get 1 single for free? I needed help. Target has everything but help.

But before I sought that assistance, while in the grooming section, I thought I might need deodorant. This should be quick. But deodorant has its own neighborhood within the Target village. Many brands, sizes, and applications—sprays, roll-ons, wipes, smears. Women, men, kids. A plethora of stink-stain cover ups. I just took a stab. Threw something in the basket and hoped for the best.

I continued looking for an employee, up and down wide aisle paths through cliffs of crap. And I happened upon a stack of lawn chairs. They were stunning. And I swear one of the chairs spoke to me. *Buy me.* I returned to the front for a wheeled cart.

Then I accidently stumbled upon a beach ball display. Although I knew a Beach Ball—Mr. Beach, my former paper customer—I never owned one. It sure would look nice next to the lawn chair. And maybe I'll get a kick out of kickin it. Here was the kicker—it was already inflated. Yes, it was time. I placed the sphere into the cart.

And then I passed an underwear display. The packages had pictures of large packaged ripped male models wearing bikini briefs. Now who looks like that? How about a little realism. Like some tubby flab hanging over the elastic waistband. And I was unaware they even made men's bikini underwear.

But my women's pair I found in the laundry nook and cranny was getting old, the color fading. And maybe I'll lose some weight. I Frisbee tossed a multi-colored pack toward the cart. It came up short against the side of the cart. I tried an underhanded finger roll. That lipped out. When I backed up to free throw length, nothing but cart.

Near the underwear department was the sock space. I grabbed a jumbo twelve-pack.

Finally, I found help—a young bespectacled guy, a generation member deep into the alphabet. He was doing banana work. Banana sales must be slow because he seemed to be dusting them. Borderline fondling. I considered his need for privacy, but I needed help.

"Excuse me. Do you handle stuff beyond bananas?"

"Sometimes."

"Does the toothpaste buy 3 get 1 free mean I have to buy 3 shrink wrapped threesomes? Or, is the free one already inside the shrink wrap?"

He seemed confused. I explained if I must buy three shrink wrapped threesomes to get another threesome free, I would own twelve large tubes of toothpaste. I don't have the warehouse space. And how long before toothpaste doesn't paste? And how long do teeth last?

He said he didn't know.

I asked what he didn't know?

How long tooth paste pastes.

What about tooth life? He didn't know. (Don't they train these people?)

What about my original question?

What original question?

I glared. Then he began to cry. And sobbed that he didn't know anything. I hugged him with consoling words—there, there, it'll be OK. You'll learn.

No, I won't, he said. I don't work here.

I went with the twelve tubes.

That was it. I was done and made my way toward checkout. It was a hike. Target should consider light rail. On the way, I grabbed a mini stapler, a Prince T-shirt, a plastic pumpkin, and some clothes pins.

While I stood in line, the woman ahead of me had a pair of tiny tots in her cart. Wow, I thought, Target really does have everything, I must have missed the kid aisle. While waiting, I grabbed a five lb. bag of jelly beans and a 10-count pack of #2 pencils. I had a jar of NutraSweet in hand but put it back. I fought the impulse. And replaced it with an Oprah magazine.

Before I move on, a couple final stuff thoughts. Stuff isn't just physical. There's also mental stuff. And that also needs to be managed. Our finite brain space is not infinite, so a periodic mental broom and dustpan should declutter to make room for new mental stuff.

And I should at least mention shopping online. That doesn't help with less stuff, but with a simple click, it can be both efficient and effective. Pretty much everything can be ordered online. Did you hear about that Amazon order for a 2,000-mile border wall?

PEOPLE

"No man is an island; except when he's having a bath."
--Norman Lovett

When I hear the word *investment*, it usually triggers a mental connection with a financial decision. But it also brings to mind relationship decisions. Who and how much time and effort should I invest into a relationship? To what level of intimacy and commitment?

That may sound presumptuous. As if it is purely my decision to immerse into people engagements. There is the reciprocity variable. To what extent does the other person care to invest in a relationship with me.

Some relationships are not, at least initially, either of our choices. They're dealt cards. Whether we want each other in our life or not, we get each other. Like family. Co-workers. Or my paper route customers. And so it is what it is.

An aside. I love that expression—*it is what it is.* It delivers a strong hint of mature acceptance. Don't fight what you can't change. But to me, the real allure of the expression is it's a variation of etcetera, efficiency word tools to conclude a topic without toiling further to explain.

For example, *the dealt card* relationships topic could conclude with the *it is what it is.* It could, but I'm going to extend this dealt card topic further into one group—neighbors. Why? Because I selfishly have a couple of stories I want to share.

Of course I've never chosen a neighbor. They just show up near my living space. Ergo-dealt cards. My simple philosophical approach to my *dealt cards* and actually, most people, has been to accept them and play nice with them. Or, try to avoid them.

Neighbors are primary recipients of my avoid approach. In fact, my best neighbor, an elderly bachelor, is a feel-good story example. Our compatibility was a two-way street, and not just because we lived on a two-way street. We both embraced avoidance. During our eleven-year physical proximity, we had never spoken. When he died, I lost not only a great neighbor, but also a close friend.

But neighbor avoidance is not entirely possible. So, I try to play nicely with them for my usual selfish reasons. Because someday I might need to borrow a cup of sugar. Now I've yet to have that need, but I've heard stories. I don't want to be that neighbor refused a cup of sugar. Not the legacy I want.

In suburbia, neighbor relationships are frequently about side yard compatibility. My current yard buddy relationships are pretty good. Fred never mows his lawn and while others complain, I refrain. Or the other extreme, George. He has a lawn cleaning service. And I've seen him with grass tweezers. He once handed me twelve leaves. Told me they were mine, blown into his yard. How thoughtful, I said. You shouldn't have. I thought I'd lost them.

***

Now to my first story. The relationship with my dead neighbor's replacement got off to a rough start.

My yard debris brush pile had grown to a sizable presence. Given the natural contents of the pile, I assumed it would naturally disappear. But it seemed reluctant to go away. One day, as I admired the accumulation, my new neighbor appeared. He asked me what plans I had for my debris pile. I thought it an odd ice breaker, but maybe, like myself, he found the creation interesting. Perhaps even amusing.

Innocently, I told him I intended to remove it, but it was one of those tasks that just kept getting pushed back by more urgent matters, an explanation I assumed he could no doubt relate to. I mean, who couldn't? Well, apparently his wife couldn't. He told me she thought my brush pile was an eyesore.

Wow. An eyesore? That had never occurred to me. This was nature's debris—fallen tree limbs, leaves, dead flowers, bush trimmings. Throw in a couple eggshells and it's a compost. Now who would attack a compost? Then it got weird. He gave me removal advice. If I just worked at it a couple hours a week, he suggested, by summer's end it's gone.

He clearly preferred candor as a bonding style. So, although I'm Tom, I became frank.

I said you wanna talk eyesore? Every day I get to look at your bright orange and red synthetic plastic replica of a McDonald's McKids Playhouse. (It might have been a thingamajig. If so, an ugly thingamajig.) That my good friend I continued, isn't an eyesore, it's visual pollution.

And those two miniature, ambulatory, whining, screaming, obnoxious little things I must listen to every day? Let me guess, are those your kids? And that non-stop yip-generating four-legged critter I assume is your dog? Well sir, those aren't earsores. They're audio pollutants.

Tom would have concluded by saying the brush pile *is what it is.* But being frank, I finished by telling him to go fuck himself. And ditto his wife.

Not really. I'm not frank. I'm Tom. And I'm a wimp.

For neighbor bonding, I thanked him for sharing his wife's concern and his helpful cleanup suggestion. I'll get right on it. Welcome to the neighborhood. If you ever need a cup of sugar, I'm here for you.

***

Here's a more interesting memorable neighbor experience.

My young couple neighbors were engaged in a bathroom remodeling project. As I discovered one early morning. It was late fall, still dark, my coffee in hand, I wandered into my backroom porch. Their re-do had yet to cover their bathroom window.

Their bathroom lights were on and into that shade-less space I unintentionally looked at the female segment of their couplehood. She appeared to be involved with what I'll describe as some sort of female magical primping. More important and relevant, she was naked.

Or at least I think she was naked. But I wasn't sure. I wasn't totally awake and my eyes weren't the best. I squinted. I really squinted. This may have been a personal best squint. But I still wasn't sure. Until I confirmed her bareness with the help of my binoculars.

This created a dilemma. Should I tell them to cover their window? Is that my role as a good neighbor? And how do I bring up that awkward topic? I pondered this for several mornings positioned behind my newly purchased tripod and high-powered telescope.

Luckily, the issue resolved itself. The neighbors covered their window without my involvement. But what remained unresolved was how to get a refund for my expensive telephoto equipment return.

***

Unlike "dealt card" people, friendships provide investment choices and decisions.

I belong to a Leadership Club. We're an old group of friends who gather frequently for intellectual stimulation and shared philosophical enlightenment. The idea was inspired by the long-ago Algonquin Round Table—a collection of men, with Dorothy Parker sitting in—they sat at a round table at the Algonquin Hotel in NYC during the 1920's, discussing philosophy, politics, religion, art, and other heady stuff while consuming massive quantities of alcohol.

It was the round concept that was the impetus to form our group. Circles are a perfect spatial space, the symbol of wholeness and harmony because circles have neither a beginning nor an end. Think bowling balls. So, we gather in circular spaces—around poker tables, at horse tracks, and taverns with horseshoe shaped bars—to get our hands around round receptacles of alcohol while getting our arms around the meaning of life.

Some recent events influenced the following correspondence from our group chairman.

Gentlemen,

Our Leadership Club membership is shrinking.

Fred left us for a strictly poker group. We'll miss his bad skill contributions. Joe is in rehab for his cocaine addiction. Sad, but at risk of insensitivity, all these years and he never once shared any coke with us. And Bill's secret private golf lessons? Unacceptably despicable. He won't be missed.

This membership decline is an urgent agenda item for our next circular gathering. So, bring some ideas about recruiting new members. Let's not panic, but should we consider women in our group?

E. Conrad Blimpington III

Chair

Well, that grabbed my attention. The future of our club was important to me. I have few friends. So, I gave the new member challenge my serious consideration.

My initial thoughts focused on how we would know if someone would be a good fit for our group? I was vaguely aware of some advice about gaining insight into someone by walking in their moccasins. But I've never known anyone who wore moccasins. And even if they did, what's the chance it's the same size? Also, how does the same foot size predict compatibility?

But I abandoned pondering compatibility. Finding someone acceptable to us wasn't our challenge. Finding anyone with any desire to hang out with us was our real stumbling block. So, my analysis shifted to our group attraction, a mental scan of our appealing assets.

Lloyd is a non-stop joke factory, entertaining because the humor is so bad it doesn't even qualify as dad jokes. Sam delivers head turning gargantuan sneezes, impressive sternutation's pre-pandemic. And collectively, we all offer eructation. I'll save you a Google—it has to do with drinking too much and wearing lampshades.

My conclusion was we are a collection of old, shallow, uninteresting men, an unappealing concoction for new membership, particularly potential women. But then I had one of those lightbulb moments. Maybe we tweak our group resume with some interesting embellishments. Make up some shit about ourselves that suggests we're people of interest. In other words, lie.

We wouldn't need to get too carried away. There's a fine line between interesting fake facts and an off-the-wall braggadocio. Maybe take the bullshit down a notch. For example, we don't say one of us was a peace medal recipient. Nominated, sure, but never won. Or did a group member sleep with Jennifer Aniston? Or Mick Jagger? No. Just good friends.

My embellished resume idea met surprising resistance. The guys expressed discomfort with lying. Was it my bad timing to suggest this during our game of liar's poker?

***

Marriage is the ultimate relationship commitment. Myself, I've struggled with marital success. I think it a result of mutually poor partner decisions.

But surprisingly, every one of my four marriages started so promisingly. Those first few days were special. But then I don't know what went wrong. I still don't. But I would like to know. Because I might want to try again.

At one of our leadership group meetings, I happened to sit next to Sam. I asked him if he had ever been divorced. When he said no, I asked if I could talk to him in private. We slid two barstools down. I shared my failed marital history, I was considering another attempt, but I was hesitant because I didn't know why the previous four ended so poorly.

What were his thoughts?

His first response was that marriage partners needed to share similar goals in life. Were my wives' goals in-sync with mine? I had to admit none were totally on board with my leisure vision.

Well, he continued, frequent open and candid discussion with each other is also important. How well did me and my wives communicate? How were my communication skills? Decent I thought. But his question did recall a discussion that was a little disjointed.

How could you eat half of that cake, my wife asked.

I said it wasn't really that challenging. You baked the cake. I found it. I just grabbed a knife and a fork. Dug into the cake and gouged out a hunk. After putting most of it on a plate, some pre-plated portions were compressed into small sphere globs and popped directly into my mouth and subsequently into my stomach.

Just get the job done as I like to say.

That's disgusting. I mean quantity. How could you eat half of a cake all at once?

Well, it's been on my bucket list for a long time.

I sensed her irritation. So, for marital harmony, I didn't point out her contribution to this escalating verbal conflict. Why did she bake such a large cake? Why did she conspicuously display it for my temptation? And what about my contribution to starving people? Eating a large quantity prevented a stale cake, whose demise, if staled, would go down the garbage chute rather than mine.

Sam agreed it was an act of sensitivity for me to withhold that last part from her. And he thought nothing in my story suggested a communication issue. He then asked me what I thought might have been reasons for my unsuccessful marriages.

I replied I've often wondered if I've had unrealistic expectations for marriage. I then told him about my paperboy mental marriage club. He agreed that may have been a tad Eden-ish.

Which was amazing he brought up Eden. Because Adam and Eve were always my benchmark. So, I shared with Sam my thoughts on my marriage template.

Living in bliss, their minimalist life in idyllic Eden, A & E were so happy, riding love and marriage together in their horse and carriage, although, without a horse, they rarely used the carriage.

Both had satisfying careers that paid below average but they managed. Eve accepted her skimpy wardrobe; Adam played less golf than he would have liked. Neither felt the need to accumulate stuff, so hoarding was never an issue.

Eve cracked up at Adam's humor. Reciprocating, Adam embraced Eve's cracked butt. Their contentment was built upon trust. And that trust naively extended to other people. They ignored warnings about door-to-door fruit salesmen. He seemed like a decent guy, and they fell for the oldest trick in the book.

That caused their eviction from their gated community. Once they got the boot, fig leaves followed. And leaf laundry. Stress entered their marriage. But they withstood these challenges. They successfully raised Cain and Abel (ly) too.

They remain my marital ideal, perhaps to a fault. So, what do you think of that Sam?

Well, at this point, I'll be honest. It sounds to me like you're just a quitter.

My immediate gut reaction was what? Quitter? I know myself well. I'm no quitter. But that was just my instinctive defensive response. Scanning my memory, some quits did surface—cub scouts, coin collecting, bowling, marbles, stamps, laundromats, and jobs. Many jobs.

So maybe I did have some quitting tendencies. I started to think that maybe I was a quitter. Boy, you think you know someone. But hold on a daggone second. Did marriage belong on my list of quits? No. I never quit a single marriage. I was fired from every gig.

Objectively though, I admit to never fully committing. I dabbled in marriage. My conclusion? I'm a blend of quit, commit, and dabble. I'm a classic Quitcomdabler.

After these thoughts, I turned back to Sam for his thoughts, and he had fallen asleep. And he calls me a quitter?

I left Sam to his slumber and slid back to the group onto a bar chair next to our group chair, Mr. Blimpington. He asked me what Sam and I were talking about. I thought he might hope we were discussing new member ideas. And I was tempted to say that. But I told him the truth. We were talking about my previous marriage failings. I was considering getting back in the ring with a new ring and was asking Sam's advice.

Mr. Blimpington asked me why would I be asking Sam for marital advice? I said because Sam has never been divorced. He said you do know that Sam has also never been married.

As I move to a new topic, I'm aware what I have shared about people decisions is not comprehensive and of suspect benefit. I guess all I can say is *it is what it is.*

LEISURE

"Doing nothing is very hard to do...you never know when you're finished."

--Leslie Nielsen

For some reason, setting goals in life gets a lot of attention. If I had a goal, and I'm not saying I did, it would have been leisure. There are several reasons why it's been an appealing focal point.

Obviously leisure is fun. Or it should be. It's also so non-specific, it can't be measured. Thus, when I claim success, there can be no dispute. Plus leisure decisions have always been easy for me. And my choices never created guilt for not getting my shit together because so many others also endorse the pursuit.

A recent Nielson Survey asked a single question: What is your goal in life? 31% had no clue. 29% said fucking off, an ad lib for leisure. 4% told Nielson to fuck off.

And further leisure support from these important people: Andrew Smart, a smart guy, in his book, *Auto-Pilot, the Art & Science of Doing Nothing*, says busyness is bad. Carl Honore, an honorable man, discusses slowing down in his book, *In Praise of Slowness.* Ernest Zalinski, an earnest guy, makes leisure supporting contributions in his book, *The Joy of Not Working.*

For the serious leisure pursuer, *How To Be Idle, A Loafers Manifesto* by Tom Hodgkinson is a must read.

But despite my success with leisure decisions, and despite all the above support for, and justification for my leisure life, occasional self-doubt has surfaced. Is there more to life than leisure? Am I missing something? So I looked behind the washer and dryer, but didn't find anything. I abandoned any further search.

Today is a historically good time for leisure pursuit. Our choices are nearly infinite. Compared to, for example, the early Romans. Their choices were limited. I can imagine the following family conversation taking place back in those days.

"Hey honey, what do you wanna do this weekend? We could take the kids to the Colosseum. Are the Christian lion feedings scheduled? Or are the gladiators fighting to their deaths performing?"

"Maybe. But how about the chariot races?"

"You know, I heard at the pyramid factory those races are fixed."

"Hmmm. Well, we might also consider the mummy wrapping event. Or we could just stay home and play one of those games making up more numerals and gods."

In contrast, we have so many opportunities for playtime. We can canoodle, count lucky stars, nitpick, string beads, tuna toss, pin butterflies, do extreme ironing, or barnstorm. And those are just top of mind.

We can also go to museums, although I'm not a big fan. But the exception is the Museum of the Weird in Austin, TX. An inconvenient location, but worth the drive. And if anyone is really into weird, just stay in Texas.

***

Gardening has recently achieved leisure status. Historically, and to add another historical tidbit to this educational book, gardening, like fishing, hunting, and baking, was survival work.

I garden. At one point I would have suggested we go down this gardening rabbit hole. But for reasons that will shortly become clear, I'm no longer welcome there. But before we dig into this growth topic, I want to clarify my gardening doesn't include vegetables. Mostly because I'm a carnivore. Plus, if I want vegetables, I can just go to the grocery store.

More history. Like leaving most taverns, I stumbled into gardening. My grass lawn had evolved into a weed lawn. Then I discovered perennials. In a sort of gardening rock, paper, scissors variation, weeds beat grass, perennials hide weeds. And perennials don't require mowing.

So, I started to replace my weed lawn with Hostas, Day Lilies, etc., thus I became a gardener. And I suppose a pretty good one. Because my plantings attracted many visitors. Not humans. Animals. They don't just stop by to admire my yard art creations, they eat it, as if it's a free buffet. They behave like animals.

I'm neither pleased nor amused. But because my animal visitors are also my neighbors, I felt the need to manage our relationship.

So initially, I kindly asked them to please not eat my stuff. They ignored me. When I begged them, they ate more. Then I groveled and they really gorged. I then began to scream at them to stop eating my shit. That had no effect either. Finally, I just flat out threatened them. Eat my art and you die. But they called my bluff.

Well, big mistake on their part. Forget neighborly relationship, they fucked with the wrong gardener. I'm not proud of what I did. And I didn't think I had it in me.

But they forced my hand. I wrote a poem.

Ode to Nature's Darlings

Songs, poems, videos often features,
nature and god's adorable little creatures.
Critters abundantly so full of praise,
But what, I ask, of their destructive ways?

Take squirrels, yes, both red and gray,
can be annoying with their reckless play.
They destroy but don't even eat,
merely mess with my shit with their feet.

Rabbits, sure, perhaps soft and furry,
but eating my stuff gets old in a hurry.
The deer browse in my yard both night and day,
my plants and shrubs, their personal buffet.

And they are all quite rude,
never a thanks for taking my food.
Moles, let's be clear, are a pain in the ass,
creepy and invisibly ruining my minimal grass.

Don't get me started on woodpeckers,
pecking trees, no, they prefer to be house wreckers.

Now I'm not an animal hater per say,
In fact, I really love the ones that prey.
Fox, for example, after a successful hunting bout,
a dead squirrel or rabbit dangling from mouth.

Coyote are lovable and hard to hate,
When they make a deer meet its fate.

So, my nasty free loaders,
live with my snubbing cold shoulders.

Now we could all get along with this simple suggestion,
eat at my neighbors to ease the congestion.

Take that you little varmints. And don't even think about borrowing a cup of sugar.

***

What is the ultimate leisure activity? A strong case can be made for sleeping. But reading would also garner many votes.

My paper route gave me the opportunity to read the daily comics. And from there, I progressed to *Mad Magazine* and then *The Onion*. All have provided intellectual food for my insatiable hunger for truth and knowledge.

There's a ton of books to read. So many choices I've found it helpful to first decide what not to read. For starters, I try to avoid anything that might make me feel stupid. Like *Beowulf, Naked Lunch, Leaves of Grass, Ulysses.* It's bad enough that they make me feel brain shorted, but just to be sure, somebody decided they're classics.

I pretty much avoid all poetry, anything written by James Joyce and the entire cadre of drunken Irish authors. They might be great writers, but their intellectual creations give me insight into what a post-lobotomy world might be like.

Now here's one that has me stumped. Tibor Fischer's book, *Don't Read This Book If You're Stupid.* I started to read it, then stopped. Then started again and stopped again. I'm still on the fence about whether I should finish it.

Let's not dwell on the negative, dark side of reading. There's a lot of good stuff. *A Confederacy of Dunces* might be my favorite book. I consider it a self-help read but I'm not sure that was the intent.

I'm sure you have your own favorites. But let me ask if you have favorite *sentences*?

Not sure how I got into this reading granularity. Probably because it's easier and thus more leisurely to examine a sentence. Through this telescopic approach, I've found many good sentences. But a great sentence makes me pause, contemplate, reflect, re-read, and savor.

My favorite sentences are organized by categories: most beautifully worded, funniest, saddest, and sickest are a few. Another favorite is the head scratcher.

A head scratcher sentence simply leaves me scratching my head wondering what it said. Here's a great example of a head scratcher by Simon Critchley from his book *Memory Theater.*

"To what extent was Nietzsche's wildly inventive, poetic, and polemical thinking contained by Heidegger's increasingly strident philosophical critique, which interpreted Nietzsche as the mere inversion of Plato and, ultimately, as a figure for our entrapment in metaphysical modes of thinking rather than a release from them?"

That produced a feeling that I made a wrong turn on my way to the bowling alley and mistakenly walked into a Yale philosophy class.

Then there's the breath holder. A breath holder sentence requires a deep breath before jumping into the deep end of this word pool. Here's a pretty good one by Tom Brokaw in his book *The Greatest Generation*, located on top of page 6:

"My father, an ambitious and skilled construction equipment operator, raced around the Midwest in his small Ford coupe, working hellishly long hours on road crews, hoping he could save enough in the warm weather months to get through another long winter back home in the small wood-frame hotel his sisters ran for railroad men, traveling salesmen, and local itinerants in the Great Plains village founded by his grandfather Richard Brokaw, a Civil War veteran who came to the Great Plains as a cook for railroad crews."

That sentence evokes the railroad crossing effect, wondering when the period caboose will appear at the end of the freight train sentence. A nice effort by Tom.

***

Recreational travel is a common leisure activity.

My trips are fewer since giving up LSD. And I travel even less since I quit flying. Air travel has always been unpleasant. But after 9/11, it has become unacceptable. The pre-flight public disrobing and groping of old men, notably myself, isn't pretty. Why not let us geezers just keep our tweezers.

The flight that finally closed the doors to my boarding life happened to be one of those rare flights that got delayed. And after I was seated, the flight captain made this announcement.

This is your captain speaking from the flight deck. Welcome aboard. Flight time to Portland will be less than a day. So just sit back and relax. Enjoy the flight. We'll be departing shortly.

But apparently the captain forgot to flip the PA switch from on to off and the following was shared with the entire plane.

Christ Jack, they forgot the luggage again. We won't leave for another hour. Now we gotta come up with a passenger story. Whadayagot for me?

Tell them the truth?

Real funny. Get serious.

OK. Peanuts are delayed in security. We used that last week. I don't know. Why don't we just leave? Say nothing. Our job is safety, not fashion. Let the passengers deal with the luggage issue. OK, how about the boarding ramps are not aligned?

The people are already boarded. Yeah, good point. That's why you're the captain and I'm just along for the ride.

Hey, I've got it. We tell them on final check off, we've uncovered flight panel dust mites. Per FAA regulation 53.2, this requires removal by special emollient personnel. They're on it as we speak. We should be airborne shortly.

***

Recreational drugs provide appealing leisure flexibility. They can be enjoyed as a stand-alone activity or a supplement to enhance other leisure activities. For clarity, I'm not talking about prescription drugs. And for simplicity, I'll skip technical drug names and just call them uppers, downers, screamers, and laughers.

Let's start at the top with uppers. Uppers can help kill the glums. But can also kill us, a downside to the upside of uppers. Feeling unsociable, bored, depressed? Nothing like a couple lines of coke to sweep those feelings away. A little toot for the snoot turns everybody and everything fascinating. Too bad coke is addictive, short lived, and has that pesky killer downside. And expensive. Someone said coke is god's way of saying you have too much money.

We can get down from the uppers by doing some downers. This is brief because I'm not a big downer guy. I can get down without help. The only allure of barbiturates is that the word has four syllables, which is always cool.

Mescaline has some screamer/laugher potential and can also add a little color to our life. And for even more intense perceptual alterations, there's LSD. Dropping acid can turn lounging on the couch into a trip without getting up. Stare at a wall and enjoy watching it melt and breathe, emitting wind tunnel sounds and a kaleidoscope of colors.

Pot is the go-to all-purpose leisure drug. It can deliver an upper, downer, screamer, or laugher. I prefer the edibles, in part because I never mastered rolling a joint. My doobies either ended up like a hat pin or an elm tree stump.

A final comment about addictions. If we become addicted, the first step to recovery is an accurate diagnosis. What exactly is our addiction? For example, Mitch Hedberg was concerned he was addicted to playing casino blackjack. But through psych analysis, he discovered he wasn't addicted to gambling; he was addicted to sitting in a semicircle.

I think Lily Tomlin makes a good point. Lily feels reality is a crutch for people who can't cope with drugs.

***

Drugs seem to naturally segue to music.

My preference is live performances. And my all-time favorite live experience was a rare shared stage by two seemingly discordant music genres. The country rock band Pork & The Ducks opened for the classical Minnesota Orchestra.

Pork, the front man for the Ducks, got his 380-pound Jell-O body shaking beneath his bib overalls, and the entire place shook. Even the classical music hoity-toity, starched shirt, highbrow audience members started head nodding, then knee slapping before everyone got out of their seats to cut a rug in the aisles with some dixie moves rarely seen in Minneapolis.

But this was even more rare. After Pork left the stage, and midway through the orchestra's performance of Handel's *Messiah*, the audience started chanting *Pork, Pork, Pork*. And he reemerged and launched into his classic "We Ain't Leavin' 'til We're Heavin." Backed by a one-hundred-instrument orchestra brought the house down. The French Horn duet with Pork was pure delight.

***

Speaking of performing arts, theater and film are perfect leisure escapes from all stresses. Although I enjoy both, I will only briefly comment on film.

My paper route allowed me at that early age to experience movies at big screen theaters. After my downtown Saturday paper payment, I went to some flicks. Most memorable were the adaptation of Edgar Allen Poe's *The Pit and The Pendulum* and Alfred Hitchcock's *The Birds*. Both were incredibly scary, and I still have the occasional nightmare. Poe and Hitchcock were two very sick guys.

Other big screen dramatic classics for me include *Duck Soup*, *Dumb and Dumber*, *Tommy Boy*, and *Borat*. Of course the ultimate, *Airplane*. And perhaps overstating the obvious, Cheech & Chong have made consistent contributions to cinematic fine taste.

The small screen shouldn't be snubbed for thought provoking productions. A few notables include *Green Acres*, *Pee Wee's Playhouse*, and *Family Guy*.

***

I'm not sure jury duty belongs in the leisure family. But I want to share my story, and I don't know where else to stick it.

I had always wanted to jury. And I finally got the call.

My jury peers and I, following a brief briefing in a basement briefing room, were led by an armed guard single file up a narrow, dark back stairway. My excitement grew with each ascending step. I had this vision of our secret entry culminating in a spectacular surprise appearance on stage to thunderous applause. Perhaps enhanced with a fog machine.

That didn't happen. We entered a somber, nearly empty courtroom. No fanfare for the judge's entry either. She was already seated. Whatever happened to the "All rise. The honorable Judge So & So presiding?" Given the circumstances, a little pomp seemed in order.

But there were a couple of nice traditional touches. Like our entry through the swinging wooden gate to our elevated wooden seats behind a wooden railing. The witness chair was next to the raised judge podium. All of that was very Perry Mason-like.

The judge spoke to us about the seriousness of our job. We must be fair and truthful. If we had any reason that we couldn't be fair, like maybe the defendant was our brother, we should divulge that. I gave the judge a thumbs up, so she knew I got the message.

This was a civil case. About money, not jail time. Some altercation had happened between an off-duty police officer and a citizen that resulted in killing the citizen. Our potential job was to figure out if this was a bad thing. I say potentially our job, because at that point, we were jury wannabe's. We might be wouldn'tbes if either attorney didn't want us to be.

While waiting for the jump ball or however these things got started, I didn't see why either attorney would object to me, an old suburban retired White guy. Plus, I had a clear point of view. The cop was guilty. I neither trust nor like cops so this should be a quick decision for everyone's benefit. The tricky part was how the dead person would tell his side of the story.

Finally, the attorneys gave each of us an envelope stuffed with cash. Just kidding. This was not Chicago, it was Minneapolis. No, what happened next was the attorneys took turns with questions directed at individual jurors. I was addressed as juror #8. I said please, call me Tom. He rudely ignored me and asked, "number 8, what are your sources of news? Where do you get information on current events?"

I considered replying objection your honor, leading the witness and clearly irrelevant. But I remembered I wasn't the attorney. My truthful response to the attorney question was the Golf Channel. Solemnity was briefly broken with some stifled laughter. Beautiful, I thought. They like me. I'm in.

My dismissal was a shock. I didn't see it coming. And it remains a mystery to me. My bet is Perry Mason would have seen my value.

***

Sport is a popular leisure activity for either participation or watching. I don't play because I'm shitty at all sports. And to watch others master a sport is a painful reminder.

The exception is golf, a much-loved sport. One unique appeal is the game is played outside, within the tranquility, harmony, and natural beauty of forested trees, lily-padded blue ponds, manicured mini-sand beaches, amid the relaxing sound of chirping birds.

But here's a dilemma. Why does a game so loved, performed in such beautiful environments, produce a consistently foul mood at conclusion?

One potential reason is the peaceful environment is disturbed when the stationary ball is mis-struck, launching the spherical orb errantly, thudding off trees as they disappear into the forested woods, scaring the songbirds to flight. Or plopping into and disturbing the calm lily covered ponds or burying and making a mess in the pristine sand beaches.

And what frequently follows these mishits is a spontaneous loud litany of crude profanity-laced verbal spewing of frustration. These sounds reverberate throughout the golf course, further disturbing the ambiance. Golf has traditionally been considered a gentleman's game. But like lost golf balls, the gentlemen have also disappeared.

Golf has an abundance of rules with associated penalties. But despite this plethora of rules, none address the potty mouth expletives after a mishit. Everyone just audibly letser rip. I think an additional rule to address these verbal outbursts might improve enjoyment and return some gentlemanly civility to the game.

My proposed Rule 876.2 would require a specific verbal response for each kind of mishit and an appropriate violation penalty:

- 1st violation: 1 stroke.
- 2nd: Mouth Soaped.
- 3rd: Mouth Duct Taped.

Shit Shot	Shout Out
Chunk	Darn
Shank	Dog gone it
Chilly Dip	Geez Louise
Double Cross	Jeepers
Duck-hook	For Pete's Sake
Banana	Great Caesar's Ghost
Skull	Dadgummit
Blade	Oops
Thin	My bad
Fat	Woswser
Whiff	You Pathetic Fucking Loser

***

Leisure pursuits are frequent items on bucket lists.

The history of bucket lists is interesting. The first bucket list dates to the 1930's. Residents of a small Oklahoma town were semi-buried by a dust storm. Because all the residents hated dusting, they decided to just abandon the town. They walked to California where they began picking vegetables, making a list of the varieties as they put them into buckets.

That inaugural bucket list inspired the book *Grapes of Wrath* by John Steinbeck. And from there, bucket lists went viral.

I don't have a bucket list, but I feel some sort of pressure to have one. And I've thought about some things I might include if I did have a bucket list.

Maybe have lunch with the Dali Lama? I dismissed that one. A Lama lunch would be hard work. Do I really want to climb a mountain to sit cross-legged eating granola and listen to a guru babble? I've heard that guy can flat out talk.

Another bucket drop-in thought was visit every (both) library in Alabama. Or take a selfie in front of the world's largest ball of twine.

I think the reason those ideas have not produced my action is I'm not sure they merit bucket list stature. But getting to heaven would clearly be bucket worthy and heaven just happens to be a spirituality topic we'll explore next.

SPIRITUALITY

"I once wanted to become an atheist, but I gave up-they have no holidays."

--Henny Youngman

It isn't a random decision for Spirituality to be my final big issue topic. Given I don't really know what spirituality is, it's a challenge for me to provide help on something so murky. But challenge is what I'm about and my fuzzy knowledge on previous topics haven't been an obstacle, so I'll jump right in.

Spirituality mostly invokes my mental thought of organized religions. Organized religions automatically triggers Catholic. But when I think Catholic, I don't think spirituality.

Because my Catholic religion experience was more like some sort of military boot camp. It was basic training to become a Catholic soldier of Christ. At the Confirmation culmination ceremony, I formally confirmed I was in His corner; would always have His back. Not allow Satan or any false religions to mess with Him.

The whole thing was an indoctrination of faith that Catholic was the only path delivered straight from God. I found it all a tad silly but at least it was easy. Beyond altar boy duties, I was never called into any other active duty. And thinking was never required nor encouraged.

As for other Christian religions, I don't really know what makes the various sects different, but Walker Percy, a deceased American writer, summarizes it well. Walker says Jews wait for the lord. Protestants sing hymns to him. Catholics say Mass and eat him.

***

Let's look at the Bible. The Bible seems to be a spiritual foundation reference guide for most Christian religions. But within my Catholic military experience, the Bible had more of an unclear, fuzzy, hazy presence. It just kind of hung around the periphery of my awareness. I remember Mass Missals in church, but I don't remember Bibles laying around in church pews.

Because I've never read it nor had formal Biblical instruction, I've always considered it a popular work of fiction. But now I get why it's a classic. What changed my point of view was a friend told me the Bible was the sex guru Dr. Ruth's source of liberal sexual expertise.

Here's the highlights of what I remember him telling me about Dr. Ruth's interpretation. This might not be entirely accurate because this is like a third or even a fourth-hand revelation separated by many years.

Although marriage and heterosexuality has long been the sexual norm, was that God's sole intent? The Bible suggests not. There are several examples of Biblical alternative sexual forays. Like Cain and Abel. They were incestuous cannibal brothers. Cain got carried away one day and completely ate Able.

And Moses, a bachelor, had his sexual edge smoothed by his friend Mary Magdalene. Financially challenged, double M asked Moses for a little something for her effort. So, Moses donated. And MM became the first prostitute.

Joseph and Mary were husband and wife, a seemingly traditional lifestyle. But strangely, they never consummated their marriage. Because they weren't sexually attracted to each other. In part because Joe was gay. His primary, but not exclusive lover, was Paul, a gigolo. And Mary was a lesbian. She and Mary Magdalene (it was a small world back then), a closet bisexual, had frequent sleepovers.

Roman gladiators were exhibitionists, engaging in public orgies before crowds of masturbating voyeurs. Pornography ended this.

The history of transgenders is a little more subtle. The miraculous conversion of water and bread into the blood and body of Christ is a transgender surgery metaphor.

Bestiality gets into a gray area. Empathetic to lonely sheep herder's, God created sheep. But when Noah's boat started to rock, God put a two-specie limit on his boat parties.

Pedophilia is unclear, but John the Baptist seemed to have a lot of kids over for his bath time play. The neither male nor female population was not biblically addressed. Likely because it's just too complex. And finally, sexual abstinence had a brief run with priests.

My reaction to these revelations was a one toke over the line sweet Jesus. Because I must admit when I previously heard Bible, sex never popped into my head. I had no idea it was pioneer porn.

However, this new information did cause my sexual soul searching. I realized I'd led a sexually sheltered life. And I reflected back to Lance Brzezinski's offer to orally reduce my sexual tension. Perhaps my response to him may have been a little hasty. Especially now that I know Lance's proposal would not only be my first, but also my last and only one of its kind, from a male or female, wives included.

***

Yoga is a less uncomfortable topic than biblical sex.

I'm told Yoga is spiritual-lite. It can be a standalone spiritual journey or a religious supplement—a sort of spiritual vitamin. Having only recently entered onto my spiritual radar, I've found yoga to be interesting enough to prompt my research into how it works. I'm no yoga yogi, but I've learned a few things yoga-ish.

For starters, the purpose of yoga is to retrieve our innate spiritual karma. We're born with karma, but karma is stagnant. Metaphysically, it's an inert gas. Although invisible, karma has volume. If not occasionally stirred, it can create a bloated feeling, frequently blamed on beer.

Karma is activated by sitting on the floor, barefoot, joining both big toes. The toes absorb cosmic air that gets the cosmic air ball rolling through the soul balls of our feet, and then continue up our body into our primary soul, located behind the aortic valve. Toe touching is also necessary to bridge the synapse between the right and left side of our soul. From there, the karma reverses flow in a closed loop system.

Once activated, the karma fills us with nothing, which, in essence, is the functional purpose for yoga—to serve as a Zen delivery vehicle. Zen is short for zenith, or more recently referred to as air head, the ultimate goal for our soul.

Another physical yoga ritual is to join both thumbs and pointer fingers while chanting *Duh. Duh*, when audibly repeated fights the urge to snap fingers and hum when karma starts to rock.

If yoga rituals aren't strictly adhered to, which is the role of dharma (cosmic law and order), it's just called sitting on the floor. Which is not all bad.

Apparently, karma is sometimes confused with aura. Easily done because both words contain a double a. But the difference is simple—an aura is external, karma internal. And surprisingly, karma has also been mistaken for halos. But there is no relationship—halos are merely artistic creations by painters to distinguish between real angels and frauds.

***

Returning to my Catholic roots…

I struggled early on my Catholic path; kinda lost my way. Maybe not entirely, but I think it was those endless strings of miracles that just seemed a little sketchy to me. And then it all just sort of collapsed one Sunday. On my way to Mass, rather than turning left to the church, I continued walking. It wasn't planned, it just happened. At age fourteen, I quit the church.

At that point, I had gotten comfortable quitting in general and, not to brag, was pretty good at it. My description of this church quit decision sounds smug. Perhaps flippant. But this was kind of a biggie quit. And doubts lingered. Might Heaven actually exist? Or more importantly, what about Hell? Were there handbaskets?

So yeah, this was a FOFU (fear of fucking up.) Well, who better to get some feedback on my doubts than my straight-shooting retired priest customer, Father McMurphy.

When I told Father McMurphy I had stopped going to Mass and had basically quit the church, his response was a raised eyebrow. I had not seen him deploy this move before. A raised eyebrow has always unnerved me, in part because I don't know how people do that. I also don't know what it means. But I assumed a raised eyebrow from a priest can't be good.

But he then simply asked why have I quit?

Well, I said, I found it boring. Which was true but was really just my way of easing into my explanation. And then I told him I just didn't really believe in Heaven and Hell.

I was kind of bumbling along with my response but then I remembered the redirect—a tactic I learned from Mr. Madigan, my politician paper customer—don't answer a question, redirect the question with a question. So, I asked him if he believed. Or was it just a necessary part of his priest job to go with the flow?

He said did you just do a redirect on me? Nice one. I thanked him.

Then he told me faith was an individual decision. Like all decisions, there is risk and reward. In my case, I was taking a lot of risk without any reward. Skipping Mass is a mortal sin, a one-way ticket to Hell. And don't expect a smooth ride in a handbasket—those were for pagans only—Catholics should know better.

Father McMurphy then told me he couldn't grant permission for me to blow off Mass (my adlib), but he could grant forgiveness by hearing my confession. And he could hear my confession right then and there.

Whoa. This was moving way too quick.

I did a visual scan of his house. Where's your confessional booth I asked. Unnecessary he said. I thought it was easy for you. You don't have to look a priest in the eyes when telling confessional lies. I told him I'd think about it and get back to him.

Confession was complicated. Although my actual sins escalated and became more diversified, my confessed sins had always remained stagnant. Effectively lying by omission and essentially sinning while confessing sins. It seemed a little counterproductive. And the whole confession thing seemed redundant. If God knows everything, why the need to re-state the already known?

So, I thought about Father McMurphy's confession offer. And not for a couple days or weeks, or even months. For over two years. I had turned sixteen having avoided the decision. He must have realized I needed decision help. Because one evening when I was collecting from him, he went for the confessional close. In exchange for my immediate confessional commitment, he'd reduce his price.

What? You charge?

Tommy, soul cleansing is not free. What do you think penance is for? And did you know the Latin definition of Catholicism means "nothing for free?"

I see, I said.

He then proposed a barter. In exchange for each of his confessional services, I would provide a two-week newspaper credit. I countered with one week. He countered with ten days. Plus, he'd throw in penance for free.

Deal.

I quickly reviewed my confessional strategy. Nothing sexual would be revealed. Not even mental sex. Which at that point covered it all. I began cautiously. In addition to skipping Mass for a couple years, I swore for many years, repeatedly taking the lord's name in vain. I cheated on a math test. Actually, most tests, all topics. I verbally fought with my brothers, physically with my sisters.

My plan was to stop there. But then I'll be God-damned if I didn't just lose it. And confessionally threw up. Out came coveting thy customer's wife (Mrs. Robertson, unidentified), the mental marriage club with the associated mental wife disrobing's.

I think my verbal sin regurgitation was caused by the lack of a confessional booth. Luckily, I regained control. Those were enough sins. I said that's it.

Father M's initial response surprised me. He asked if I would like a glass of wine. He must have noticed I had wet myself. Not urine. Sweat. I was a sweat mess.

He said you were an altar boy, right? So, this couldn't be your first wine taste. Altar boys drinking church wine is no secret he said, we use it as an employment perk to reduce turnover.

Well, if the substitute God thought he was gonna squeeze out more sins from me with a little alcohol, forget it. And the world wine supply was too small for me to confess to masturbation. But I did accept his wine offer, and boy,

Patrick's private wine was a serious upgrade from the church cruets fluids.

His sin feedback began with my Mass skipping. Hell-worthy he said, but now I'm cleansed. Temporarily. Pending my future behavior. He encouraged me to think of confession as a sort of Hell insurance policy.

He said my swearing was a normal response to disappointments. But he advised me not to be rude and try to keep God and Jesus out of my vocabulary.

As for my fighting, he said you certainly should defend yourself, but never initiate a fight. And never fight a female physically and more importantly, never verbally. You have no chance of winning. And finally, don't fight a schizophrenic—you'll have to take them all on.

Huh? Sorry, he said. Bad priest humor. Kind of like a dad joke.

Cheating on tests, he continued, is not a sin. Actually, it's a smart use of the classic seek forgiveness rather than permission. And coveting Mrs. Robertson isn't a sin.

What? How did you know I coveted Mrs. Robertson? Oh, come on, every guy in the neighborhood covets Mrs. Robertson. She's flat out hot. But I thought you weren't supposed to reveal confessional secrets. That's not a confessional secret. What do you think is talked about at Andy's Tavern?

Now I was pleased this wasn't a sin. But I don't think he had all the facts. My coveting was not some barroom banter. I was into some serious coveting. Continuous chronic corrupt coveting. But learning Mrs. Robertson was shared with many coveters? That took a little glow off our relationship. I thought we had something special. Was she mentally married to others? Was Mrs. Robertson a mental marriage bigamist? Or, should I step in and defend her honor?

He dismissed my mental marriage club as unrealistic fantasy. I didn't appreciate his flippancy on what I had worked hard to create. But I was pleased with Patrick's narrow view of sin. Which encouraged me to ask him what other services he offered. Like maybe a mini-Mass?

Yes, but he had a strict ten-person minimum. No exceptions. But he did offer a Sunday brunch Mass-lite at Andy's. Basics only, no communion.

Shortly after that confession, I quit my paper route. With nothing left to barter with Father McMurphy for his confessional service, that was my final soul cleansing. I never confessed again nor attended another Mass. My lost way resumed and remains lost.

REACTIONS

"Remember, if life gives you lemons, a pinch of salt and a shot of Tequila are not far behind."

--Unknown

The final decision to explore is how we react to outcomes. How things turn out because of our choices or perhaps other people's decisions or maybe just pure luck.

Results are a collection of "some's." Some good results, some bad. But regardless of the outcome, we can choose to accept what happens and get on with life or, maybe we might feel a need to respond in some other way. Maybe dwell further on the result.

Here's some of the ways I sometimes choose to respond to stuff that happens in my life.

I'll start with good results. It's simpler. Regardless of the cause of the positive outcome, I usually just do a high-five selfie. Because that good result was likely created by my superior decision or, I deserved the good fortune that randomly arrived.

But it becomes a little more complicated when things don't go so well.

Reacting to bad results from my bad decisions, I think it's healthy to not be too harsh on myself. So my frequent initial gut reaction is to seek blame externally. But then I hit the pause button. I have this sense of guilt that I should just mature-up and accept total responsibility. It's really me. My DNA. My brain. My bad.

But who chose my DNA? Who created my brain? Who made those picks? Not me. So I re-set the pause and pursue a culprit. The result was not my fault.

Now sometimes I do accept the bad outcome and just move on. But I frequently prefer to delay the move on. Wallow briefly, or longer, in a self-pity, woe is me sulk for getting life fucked. Again. And will it ever end?

But when my pity party's over, then I just get back on the horse. Really? No. I would never do that. That was humor. Why add injury to insult? Rather, I wait for the sun to shine again. If it doesn't shine, well maybe it's because it's still night—so I just go back to sleep and wait for sunrise.

***

For some of my nastier results, I may not want to sulk privately. I might want to share my misfortune with others, so they know what happened to me. But just blurting out a hard luck story is a little crude.

So, I usually go with the sulk and pout. The sulk combined with a pout are subtle sharing techniques I've found to be successful at generating a "gee, what's wrong?" inquiry. Then I can gush forth with all the messy details of how I got screwed.

***

Sometimes the sulk & pout is too subtle. If nobody asks what's wrong, I add the sigh. A well-timed, deep audible sigh, combined with the sulk & pout, is a strong hint I have troubles. And most people will respond with a "wow, what happened to you?"

***

But even the sulk, pout, sigh triumvirate can be too subtle. If no empathetic concern is expressed, I roll out the double sigh. The second sigh is a little more prolonged, combined with a droopy mouth and shoulder sag. That should do it but, if necessary, I go with the serial sigh. The third sigh addition includes an alternating downward floor glance and an out-the-window gaze. These multiple steps take a little practice to nail the ideal serial sigh timing and body language.

I've learned though that the maximum is three sighs. Beyond three can turn my listener from a "you poor thing, tell me more, how can I help?" empathizer into an "I gotta run" escapist. I've also found that my empathetic generating success with the sulk, pout, sigh is significantly diminished with those who recognize that this is my everyday normal behavior.

***

Moving along through my bad results response menu choices, I might utilize the whine.

Briefly, a whine is the verbal cousin to the pout. Whines are usually a brief, weak-emotioned discharge. Whining is generally an ineffective, pathetic, self-centered, wimpy acknowledgment that I have no control over my bad result or anything else in my life.

If so, why whine? Simple. Whining just feels good. I've always enjoyed whining. And I've gotten pretty good at it. Like when Heinz Ketchup went to the plastic squeeze bottle. Their ketchup had always been defectively too thick. But I stuck with them through their thick, absent their thin. I mastered pounding the glass bottle bottom without a wall or clothing splatter. My response to their selfish move to the squeeze? I squeeze out a whine.

***

The rant is another tool choice to deal with shit results.

A rant is a power whine. Rants extend the length, increase the verbal volume, and add more emotion into the whine. A well-articulated rant, like other emotional reactions, can be an art form. And can produce an almost Zen-like spiritual cleansing.

***

Although solo ranting is rewarding, the group rant is even more so. Like with my old altar boy buddies. You talk about ranting. Back in the day, we mastered Latin, delivered a flawless Mea Culpa, wore silly altar boy clothing stylishly, swung smoking incense urns like most people swing arms, and our genuflections were completed with the grace of a gymnast.

Then English replaced the Latin mystery. Priests began to face congregations, their sleight-of-hand magic gone. Lay people started handing out bodies of Christ like business cards. With our expertise dismissed, we easily fell into the group rant. But always in Latin.

***

But did we complain? No. Because nothing would change. And change is the goal of the complaint—try to reverse a bad result caused by decisions made by others. For example, my cable provider.

Every year they try to slip their price increase by me. When I catch their treachery, I call a supervisor. But I don't whine or rant. I deliver a firm complaint with an ultimatum: rescind the rate increase or I'm a gone customer. This always starts a back-and-forth verbal tussle. The supervisor pushes back with a formidable stern resistance. Until finally, because I'm a valued long-term customer, they won't raise my rates.

That was the tradition. But recently? I fire up one quit threat and higherup collapses, folds and immediately approves my current lower rate. There was no battle, no pushback. Ergo, no reward or satisfaction. This was a hollow victory. And one I could not accept. I declined the lower rate.

But I still wasn't done. I said I needed a breakout of my bundled pricing. What was I paying individually for TV, internet, and my landline? (Yes, I still have a landline. Why? Who knows.)

Her response? Spontaneous laughter. Lengthy, loud, genuine guffaws. So genuine, it was infectious—I cracked up as well. She said that's precious. I said thanks. We had so much fun laughing, after we caught our breath, we made a lunch date.

Cable experienced a tiny sample of my complaining bandwidth. They escaped my full wrath. They were lucky. Because I can't tell you how many service providers I've fired. Can't tell you because I've never fired one. Why would I? I have no desire nor idea how to replace them. But that doesn't mean I won't. Let God strike me dead if I don't do so in the future. Or start the necessary research process for replacing them. At the very least, give serious thought to thinking about all of this.

***

The difference between the whine, rant, and complaint is sufficiently subtle to confuse. For example, I complained to Queen, the telephone recipient of my bad trash-hauling service complaint. She verbally slapped me. Told me she didn't have to put up with my whines or my rants. Huh. I thought I was complaining. I thanked her for her clarification. She appreciated my thanks, and then she said please, call me

Queenie. Just don't call me late for dinner. God that was funny. We're now friends.

***

Swearing is an appropriate response to an unfortunate result. One of the nice things about profanity is the flexibility. Potty mouthing can be a stand-alone reaction or an enhancement to any response. Properly deployed, swear words can be an artistic garnish for the sulk, pout, sigh, rant, complaint entrées.

Despite its popularity, swearing has long been disparaged. Considered low brow. A crude, immature, lack of emotional control outburst. For me, that just adds to the appeal.

And I'm not alone. The British researcher Emma Byrne states we should listen more closely when someone swears, because chances are they're telling us something important.

Emma expands:

"Deployed skillfully, swearing can be cheeky, funny, outrageous, or downright offensive. Profanity can help withstand pain, diffuse stress. It turns out it's fucking useful. We're often told that swearing isn't big or clever, it's a sign of a stunted vocabulary or limited intellect. But I can assure you that swearing can be intelligent and powerful. It can be fucking amazing. So, I do hope you might give it the fucking respect it deserves."

I toilet tongue somewhat frequently but avoid becoming a muck-spout.

***

Our concluding response option is the full-blown meltdown. Although I present the meltdown last, it isn't necessary to go through the above sequential steps to deploy it. Sometimes I go directly down into a melt.

Like swearing, meltdowns have a negative stigma. Pooh-poohed, to use the professional vernacular. But meltdowns are a natural response to shit. So, I say let it blossom, uninhibited, without guilt. It just seems healthier to get it immediately out of the garage.

The meltdown repertoire is nearly endless and is a personal preference. Some of my most common meltdowns include crying, screaming, floor flopping, dog kicks, hair pulls, finger-in-mouth stretch, wall head beat, shoe throw, palm-to-forehead thump, arm bite, pogo stick-like serial up and down jumps. And sometimes I'll throw in some swear for verbal flair.

Although most of my meltdowns are spontaneous, I admit, embarrassingly, that I have utilized the staged, manipulative meltdown. I call it the manip-melt. The purpose of a manip-melt is to manipulate someone into more than just a hug response. I might use it to induce a "you scare me, let me help you" reaction. Success getting that actual desired action requires a decision of which meltdown tools work best for a specific manipulation goal.

For example, crying is really a mini-melt. Kind of a beginner ploy. Crying once got a teacher to upgrade my D-minus to a D. But simple crying has never been successful at getting someone to give me their seat on a full commuter train. So, I add a floor flop and a scream. Success has been geographic. No go in Tokyo. Zero floor space for the flop. Forget New York City. No strange behavior even turns a head. Any manip-melt in Chicago is more likely to get a bullet than a seat.

But Minneapolis? Always successful. And I've since found no need for a manip-melt. If I just ask someone if I could have their seat, they oblige. Minnesota nice is remarkable.

***

Before closing this out, I want to mention moping. Beyond recognizing it as a response tool, I won't expand further. Because I don't know what it is and I don't think I've ever moped. Or at least I've never been called a moper or a mope. But it's on my bucket list.

I've weighed in on physical and mental health, money, where to live, stuff, relationships, leisure, and spirituality. I think that pretty much covers life's biggies. I have no more wisdom, advice, stories, thoughts. Now if anything I've offered has been useful to you, that makes me feel good. But I must say that I'm a little surprised.

PART 3
POST POST-PAPER ROUTE

HEAVEN

"Go to Heaven for the climate, to Hell for the company."
--Mark Twain

Unfortunately, I've died. I know. Pretty sad. More so given I didn't see it coming. But the upside is I'm up in heaven. And I really didn't see this unexpected arrival arriving.

For starters, I never really believed the place existed, and if it did, small chance I would get in. But my entry was not a reward for my good behavior. Nor a reward for my tenure as a Catholic. There is a formal process for access through the pearly gates.

That formal entry approval process I will share with you, having been cleared by the top dog himself, God. Yes, if you had doubts, He's real. We've met. And I must say, He's actually not a bad guy. (And his preferred pronoun is Guy, with a capital G.)

Heavenly membership is decided by a four-spirit committee—Jesus, Mary, Joseph, and the Holy Ghost. It's a simple majority rule with God as the tie-breaker. My vote was close, 3-2 in my favor. I've always been pretty good at math. Clearly, God tipped the scales for my benefit.

What was not revealed was how specific members voted. My guess is Jesus was a likely no vote. I've been a little harsh on the Son. And I suspect Ghost was not in my corner. If true, the Ghost can kiss my ass.

Anyway, things are nice here. Spacious, comfortable accommodations. I have a private puff within a shared cloud. St. Peter looks good. He's dropped some weight. But those are just a couple details. What is really fascinating is my conversation with God.

Our meeting happened by accident. I was cloud hopping one day when I ran into a partially opened door. When I knocked, someone said come in. And there He was, seated behind a desk, a GOD name plate atop.

"OMG."

"Yes? Come in, come in. Sit down. What brings you to town, Tom?"

Before I share the details of our visit, I had this initial feeling or sense He was lonely. I assume He's so intimidating, nobody visits Him. And likely He's also bored. Once He set things up in those hectic first few days of non-stop creating, He's probably outsourced everything and has nothing to do. Kind of sad when I thought about it.

Anyway, initially we talked sports, weather, and family. But then I thought, what the Hell, go ahead and ask Him why he approved my entry to His kingdom. I mean, not only did I not follow the confessional guidelines, my entire resume was a little, I don't know, tarnished?

With a flip of his hand and a subtle head shake, He poo-pooed the whole confession thing as a bunch of Catholic fake news.

His thumbs up vote for me was a combination of things. My cloud interest was compatible with the neighborhood. My leisure-focused lifestyle aligned well with His original Heaven blueprint—ad infinitum leisure. And He told me He also saw a little of Himself in me.

"Really?"

"Oh yeah. Like yourself, I've always struggled with decisions. It wouldn't be so bad if there weren't so many of them—Mental and physical health, money, where to live, stuff, people, leisure, spirituality. Non-stop decisions. They're a pain in the ass."

"You got that right, God. Do I call you God?"

"My friends just call me G. Just don't call me late for dinner." He cracked up.

"Um, G? Lose that one. It's become an embarrassing groaner. And unbecoming of you."

"Thanks for the heads-up, Tom. Or do you prefer Thomas?"

"Call me Tom. Just don't call me late for dinner." He groaned.

"Here's another part of you I saw in myself. Or a part of me I saw in you. Anyway, your mental marriage club creation. That showed initiative. Like my world creation and this heaven club. I thought my cloud gang could use a little more initiative. And I really liked that you were a paperboy. I had always wanted to be a paperboy."

"No kidding."

"Oh God yes."

"Are you talking to me or yourself?"

"What?"

"Never mind. Continue."

"Absolutely I wanted a paper route. And I think I deserved one. I mean, I created most of the news. So why don't I go ahead and just deliver that news. Plus there was just something kind of romantic about a paperboy's life. I mean paperperson. Forgive me, I'm still adapting to the current correct gender usage."

"What? Are you saying I should forgive you? Isn't forgiveness your job? And can't you just forgive yourself?"

"Don't split hairs with me Tom. What's important is I wasn't lucky enough to get a paper route."

I thought to myself that's too bad. Although I hadn't spoken, He said thanks. I still struggle with His mind reading. He'll never know, but I find it annoying. It triggers some bad memories of former wives.

Now that I was secure as a member of His club, and we had bonded, I thought the Big Guy might benefit with my candor.

"G, are you aware you're losing fans? People are seriously questioning your existence. And your Heaven and Hell are also suspect."

"You're kidding."

"Let God strike me dead if I am. No, ignore that. I'm not messing with you."

"Do you have any ideas how I might stem this doubt tide?"

"Yes. Word needs to get back to the populace that all of this isn't just a pipe dream."

"Maybe you have a point."

"Bingo!"

"Shit. Forgot we were playing." (Well, He is old.)

"How might this be accomplished?"

"Easy. We start a newspaper. Guttie (Guttenberg) is here and could design a heavenly printing press. And with my paperboy experience, I could set up a worldwide paper route distribution network."

"That's a great idea. I think. Despite some FOFU, I'm going to approve this, with two conditions. First, all content needs to be run by me before going to print."

"Oh, for Christ's sake, you're not going to God damn it all are you?"

"No, no, relax. I just want to make sure I'm portrayed as a good guy God. And no bad hair day pictures."

"What's your second condition?"

"I get a paper route."

***

OK, that's all I got. It's a wrap. Not just this part, everything. Best of luck with your decisions. Thanks for hanging out with me.

Paperboy has left the building.

AUTHOR NOTES

I had fun creating *Paperboy*. And I hope you had some fun reading it. That was my primary intent. Provide a little comic relief. A laugh, giggle, chortle, smile, or just a smirk.

Humor has been prominent in my life and I think it also has sufficient universal relevance to justify my indulgence into this little extended humor analysis.

Analysis infers some deep thinking. So am I a deep thinker? Not quite. My analytical dives are shallow. Not deep enough into any topical body of water to require scuba gear. I'm more of a toe dipping analyst.

***

E.B. White said that analyzing humor is like dissecting a frog. Few people are interested, and the frog dies of it. But despite that, there have been many attempts to examine and try to understand and explain the nature of what is funny and why we laugh.

Two themes are common within these explorations.

Many theorists maintain there is a strong relationship between humor and pain. The association suggests that we use humor as a way to escape or cope with some form of underlying hurt we feel. The other dominant theory is the strong role that incongruency plays within humor. The surprise end to an expected conclusion. Some think that all humor has some component of incongruency.

As I examine my personal humor relationship with pain, I don't know if I'm trying to escape some hidden pain in my life. Probably. But if so, I'm unaware. I suppose if I want to find out, I should consult a professional head person. To this point, my curiosity hasn't been that compelling.

Incongruency? No question it has a large presence within my humor world. But I don't like the word. It feels a little too hoity-toity for my comfort. I prefer absurdity. Absurdity is my word and humor god. It permeates my entire relationship with humor- recognition, appreciation and creation. And the more absurd the better.

But if you actually read this book, you already knew that.

This concludes my humor analysis. Not because I have nothing further to say about it. But because any further analysis would validate E.B. White. I would bore you and I also don't want to get labeled as a serial frog killer.

Although I now depart from humor analysis, I want to continue to explore absurdity. But not absurd humor. I want to focus on absurdity that is non-humorous. Absurdity that is not funny.

***

I had a relatively young awareness of things that were absurd but not funny. Things that I unlikely initially processed as such. Unlikely my young brain filed them into a folder labeled absurd not funny. More likely it was information that probably just confused me. Like why can only Catholics get to heaven? How could Columbus have "discovered" America? I wasn't clear what was amiss, but something just didn't seem quite right.

Fast forward to today, 2026. Absurd non-humor examples are easily recognized and identified.

Here are a couple that come quickly to mind. Not presented in any order of importance, nor would everyone even agree they are absurd. But to me, they all have a strong whiff of absurd odor.

Why isn't legal assistance for death with dignity provided as a universal right?

Supreme Court judges have no sunset on their tenure even while some rule on matters based upon their political slant, answering to no one for their decisions. And why only nine members? Wouldn't more voices be more likely to get justice right?

How did wealth inequality reach today's absurd disproportion? While a million people globally experience hunger, one person has a current net worth of over $852 billion dollars. Something is out of whack.

What has happened to the media that historically delivered news with minimal political or social slant? Where have you gone Walter Cronkite? How have fake news and conspiracy theories established such a strong foothold? Who are the sources and what are their motives?

Congressional divisiveness. Climate change. Pandemics. Nuclear weapon proliferation.

Most absurdity fixes are directly controlled by government institutions. As individuals, we might have some influence on decisions, but we can't remedy the absurd issue.

But we do control things that impact some absurdities.

We control which government leaders represent us.

Our choice of personal values that guide our behavior. How important we hold values of decency like kindness, respect, empathy, acceptance, assistance, decency.

How we treat our fellow human beings is our decision.

And here are our contributions to the current absurdities.

We chose a character as our president with no evidence of character. A documented habitual liar void of decency who encourages divisiveness for his benefit. The odor he emanates is remarkable for the power of its stench.

We withhold our acceptance, kindness, respect, caring, empathy from those of us with different skin color, gender, body shape, age, sexual preference/identities, disabilities, ethnicity, cultural heritage, religions.

We have a divisive, disruptive disagreement with those with a different political/social point of view.

None of this absurdity, governmentally or individually controlled, is particularly new. But the list of absurdities seems to be growing daily. It almost seems the distinction between absurdity and reality continues to erode. What was at one time absurd is now almost the norm and what was once reality is now absurd.

Hopefully the current ICE behavior in Minneapolis as I write this will reach the bottom of our absurd plummet.

***

These collective behaviors cause me to scratch my head with the stunning lack of decency but more so, the absence of logic. Which prompts me to seek clarifying insights from resources who have examined our illogical absurdity.

Kelly Clancy, the author of *Playing With Reality*, discusses the expanding presence of a win-lose, or zero-sum thinking perspective among many of us.

"People tend to believe that all resources are limited, even when this is not the case. An isolationist might oppose immigration because they think immigrants "steal" from a fixed number of jobs, not realizing that immigrants also create new jobs. A fervent nationalist might believe that any progress made in another country translates to their own being worse off, rather than sharing in the benefits. A racist might conclude that any assistance given to other groups translates to a loss of their own."

"This pervasive view undermines trust and hinders the cooperation so crucial to humankind success. Zero-sum thinking results in antagonism between individuals and groups. It's clear what people believe makes a difference in how they behave. Zero-sum arguments abound in political rhetoric, and some bring that mindset to the polls."

***

The ancient Greek philosophers wanted to influence others to accept their philosophical beliefs. And to improve their success, they analyzed how people are influenced. That produced an influence model that Steven Covey reproduced in his book, *The 7 Habits of Highly Effective People.* I'll adlib Covey's adlib from the Greeks how people are influenced.

1. Ethos (Credibility): Do I trust you? Do you speak the truth? Do you know what you're talking about?
2. Pathos (Emotion): Do you understand me? Do you care about me?
3. Logos (Logic): If I trust you, if I feel understood and cared about, I then might consider your logic.

All three steps are important, but the sequence is most important. Jumping immediately to logic without establishing trust, understanding and caring doesn't work.

***

Frank Bruni in his book, *The Age of Grievance*, examines the strong presence of how we individually and collectively feel we have been grieved.

***

Gallup began polling citizens in 2006 about their level of national government trust. That first poll had Americans at the top of the polled countries. In 2023, Americans were dead last.

***

There is also a thing called a *Violation Theory*. It says we have a sense of "how the world ought to be." And how we feel threatened and violated when something is viewed as wrong.

***

Those comments provides some insight into how some of us think and behave. And I'll tag on with a couple of my thoughts.

Some of us who lack trust in government leadership, think we are not going in the right direction, feel misunderstood, not cared about, and aggrieved are perhaps not doing as well economically as they once did.

I call them the *Whadaboutme's*.

As they struggle, they see government programs and resources helping other portions of our population but not them. Some may feel that nobody has ever helped them. They have had to earn everything. And maybe some also believe God only helps those who help themselves. Those other recipients of assistance haven't earned that help.

And maybe they find it easier to ignore some of their personal values when they enter the polling booth.

I don't judge them.

There's another group I'll call the *Allaboutme's*.

I'll stereotypically and perhaps unkindly describe them as privileged white educated wealthy suburban people. Who are certainly not struggling.

I do judge those *Allaboutme's* who selfishly helped move our guy into the big white house on Pennsylvania Ave.

Shame on you.

***

To this point, I've primarily described our absurdities as illogical. But as a reminder of my shallow analytical plunges, I'll now also summarily characterize our non-humorous absurdities as ugly evidence of a lack of Quality.

And now I want to take a shallow dive into Quality. But first, a little biographical background as an introduction.

I'm a Baby Boomer. And as a member of that generation, I shared the rejection of much of our parent's way of life and mentally embraced the allure of the *Dawning of the Age of Aquarius* alternative lifestyle.

The dreamy vision of living with my hippy peers on a commune. Getting high, making love, not war, growing long hair and hybrid rutabaga's. Talking smart about how we'll save the world as we toss a frisbee around naked and learned to play a sitar.

This was a mental embrace. I never actually acted upon that romantic vision. It was unrealistic. I knew I'd never learn to play the sitar.

But as I pondered what I wanted to be when I grew up, I stumbled upon the book by Robert Pirsig, *Zen and The Art of Motorcycle Maintenance*.

Pirsig takes a motorcycle road trip cross-country from Chicago to the West Coast. He alternates his narrative between his physical observations and his mental analysis in pursuit of the concept of Quality.

What exactly is Quality? What makes something of Quality and, the opposite, something lacking Quality? He found it difficult to define, but the presence is readily recognized, as is the ugliness in its absence.

He further states that Quality is the proverbial two-sided coin. One side is Quality, the flip side Caring. Quality doesn't exist without Caring.

Quality has no boundaries. Its presence or absence permeates everything, everybody, everywhere. Our domestic issues aren't local. They're world-wide. And Quality and Caring are within our individual control.

But our absurdities expose it's ugly absence.

***

I suppose now is a good time to reveal my motivation for adding these notes to my *Paperboy* story.

Our present absurdities has moved me along a continuum from unconcerned, to worried, to disturbed, to fear. My fear is that our current direction is creating a dire future for humanity.

Do I sound like an alarmist? And maybe that question brings up the broader question of just who am I?

Despite what you might think, I don't consider myself a bleeding heart ultra-liberal. Okay, maybe I have some leanings in that direction. Perhaps my heart bleeds more liberally than most. And I also don't think of myself as a gooder guy than many. Okay, maybe a little gooder than some. I also don't possess a bunch of answers and solutions to my opinionated concerns. Nor do I presume to think I will convert anyone's opinions.

So who am I? I'm privileged. Privileged to be able to write a book analyzing stuff. Most humans aren't in this position. Some can't write. Some can't even talk, walk, or feed themselves. Many, too many, are just trying to stay alive. And some don't survive age 16.

Those are the *Whadaboutthem's*.

Who else am I? I'm just your everyday romantic. And as a romantic, perhaps I end up like Joni Mitchell's future vision, cynical and drunk, boring someone in some dark café.

If I haven't bored you sufficiently yet, I'll try harder. (But I prefer to skip the café and find a dark dive tavern.) But until and if then, I retain my romantic hopes.

Although our global village problems and challenges are complex, as a romantic, I think we possess all the necessary resources—intellectual, financial, raw materials, etc.—to fix any complex problem.

And individually we have the capacity to replace the absurdities with a collective focus on values that will bring the beauty of Quality into our individual and collective lives.

I don't think John Lennon's dream that at some point the world will come together as one is a pipe dream.

My thoughts are shared within the messages delivered by a children's book, *The Everybody Club*, that all of us adults could learn from. (Is this a shameless plug for an author I know? It needs no plug.)

To this point I'm pretty proud of myself for mostly ignoring that elephant in the room. That absurd winner of the 2024 U.S. presidential election.

But now I'll remove my gloves. He exhibits the largest example of the ugliness in the absence of Quality that is the essence of absurdity without humor.

He's also lucky he didn't grow up in Paperboys neighborhood. He would've gotten his wealthy privileged pretty boy ass kicked every day until he learned not to manipulate, bully, or mess with those struggling to defend themselves.

Fuck you trump. And your buddy putin. The omission of caps are intentional.

ACKNOWLEDGEMENTS

There are so many people I'm indebted to for providing me their generosity and loving encouragement any writer or anyone could hope for.

Thanks to Pat Kovar, Linda Hayen, Nancy Loewen, Pat Sfondilas, and Todd Hayen for their helpful feedback to my early renditions of this book.

I'm grateful to members of the Twin Cities Fiction Writers Jody Schmiesing, Greg Tripoldi, John Harrigan, Karl Jorgenson, Robert Beck, Kristin Harley, Elizabeth Neiman, Candy Almquist, Avron Gordon, Susan Stradiotto, Sophia Johnson, and Terry Faust, for their close readings, deep thinking, and beneficial input.

My gratitude runs deep to author Annabelle Lewis for her consistent, thorough, expert advice, guidance and wise council. Ares Jun for his artistic design. And special thanks to Michael MacBride at Salty Books. Without Michael's expertise this book would not exist.

I've decided to take this opportunity to extend gratitude beyond my writing world and into my personal life. A very belated thank you to some long ago special adults from my youth who pointed me in the right direction when I was lost but didn't know I was lost-Sal Dispensa, Charlie Pisoni, Jerry Miller, and Charlie Silverman.

Dave Schor for his ongoing presence within my continuous grief cocoon since Carissa left my life. Sheila Fitzgerald stepping in to help me retain what minimal grip I had on sanity at that time. Veronica Vodak for all of her incredible irreplaceable help to our family, enabling Phillip to expand his experience with more of life's pleasures despite his significant disabilities.

What great fortune for me to have a lifetime of friendship and love with my siblings Juanita, Sue, and Ray. How lucky we were to have Claire as our incredible Mom.

My children, Carissa, Phillip, Todd. Where do I begin to express my joy and wonder with their brilliant presence in my life. I can't. Any effort diminishes their incredibleness.

The kids and myself have had the good fortune to have Linda as their Mom, performing double duty filling in the gaps of my parental inadequacies.

My grief has no end with the absence of Carissa, Claire, Juanita, Scot, Glen, Mary Lou, and Pat Chamberlin.

Everyone mentioned here and others that should be, have a connecting thread. They all exemplify Quality.

ABOUT THE AUTHOR

Glenn Hayen

When I remove my writing cap, an ideal day might find me engaged in my favorite activities. Like attempting to create some land art in my Eden Prairie, Minnesota backyard. Or maybe eating at a mom and pop diner. Perhaps listening to live music at an intimate neighborhood tavern, viewing a theatrical performance at a small venue, laughing with a comic on stage, visiting an artist studio, browsing shelves at an independent book seller.

In other words, exploring the diversity of interesting people, places, and artists that make the Twin Cities such a unique urban environment. And not just in the city neighborhoods. Day trips into the lush beautiful Minnesota countryside, discovering small towns and their unique culture.

I'm privileged and lucky to indulge my enjoyment and support for the small businesses and artists who deliver Quality while escaping the corporate and political purveyors of their ugly absence of Quality.

www.ingramcontent.com/pod-product-compliance
Lightning Source LLC
Chambersburg PA
CBHW030916060726
47591CB00005B/1569
9781964354101